Into The Shadows

Marie Jones

ISBN: 978-1-326-50580-6

PublishNation
www.publishnation.co.uk

For the three loves of my life...
my husband, my daughter and my son

Chapter One

I've never really been an impulsive person, daring to try new things. I'm not the girl you would secretly admire, dream, envy you were more like. No, I'm the one whose doing the dreaming, the envying, the desiring. In my whole twenty nine years to date, I'm ashamed to admit that I've never, not once, leapt into the big unknown; ready to grasp whatever was hurtling towards me.

I live a very tidy, organised and, yes, bland life. I know that, I'm so aware of that. I wish my days were full of multicoloured lights and pictures and moving spheres. I wish for ... oh I don't know, just to feel *something, anything.* Dare I even say it... love? And yet, just saying that word aloud, and I'm breaking out in a cold sweat. The thought of that uncontrollable emotion getting ahold of me makes me literally shudder all over.

So, taking all this into account, brutally accepting what I am, I'm now having to face the stark, simple truth - I've lost control of my mind. I must have, completely, to be even contemplating this, to allow this idea to gain momentum to the point I have this crazy tingling excitement coursing through my body.

Because you can't exist, you can't. The idea is preposterous, ridiculous! No, I need to push this insane urge away, reject it out of hand. Be grateful for my safe, predictable world I've safeguarded around myself.

Yet, yet...

I feel this ... pull to you, a complete and utter stranger, and it's so strong I'm not sure how I can resist it. And that is a very new phenomena for me. It's like I can hear you calling out to me to return, come back, and I'm finding myself obeying you. My goodness, is this what crazy, irrational behaviour feels like, this trapping of your mind?

I'll come. I will. I'll try and help you... if you want me too.

1

But I'll be honest with you. I'm sitting here, feeling so inadequate. I'm scared, even, of my own shadow, for pity's sake. I wish, oh how I wish I was stronger, more confident, more sure of myself. I have no idea why you've chosen me. I don't get it, I really don't. Do we know each other, from some distant time or place? I definitely don't recognise you ... but maybe that's just down to my appalling memory.

I do have to secretly confess to something - this feeling of being driven to do this is quite intoxicating, liberating even.

So this is me, right now. I'm confused, yet clear-headed. Irrational, yet focused. I'm packing my practical navy suitcase, while looking down amazed at what my own shaking hands are doing. I'm nervous, but … excited. So excited. As if I'm waking from a long dreamless sleep, where up to now I've been conducting my life. That until this moment, I have been hovering in the safety of the sidelines and now, finally, I am stepping out towards centre stage.

So wait for me, please, because I'm coming.

Chapter Two

The last of the sinking sun was slanting through our dusty venetian blinds, as we stood together at the kitchen sink. *I need to clean them,* I thought absently as I dutifully took the next plate from Nina, my flatmate, all the while aware I was about to be lectured in grand style.

And yes, here it comes. Eyes round as saucers, mouth dropping to skim the floor, a stare that could burn holes into the plate I was holding.

'Sorry ... sorry I think you need to repeat that...because just for a moment there it sounded like you were "on a hunch",' here, Nina's soap covered hands flapped wildly around her, spraying us both with sparkling bubbles, 'taking unpaid leave, packing a suitcase and heading back to Dingle. And this very sudden, and frankly insane idea, is because of some random photo you took there last month, on some beach I can't remember the name of-'

'Inch beach', I supplied, in a voice not quite my own.

'Riiigght ...so good to have that confirmed.' Came the sarcastic shot back at me, her eyebrows raised so high they were practically swallowed up by her fringe. 'Where was I? Oh yes, to find some unknown woman who appeared like some genie on your photo. About right?' I nodded, biting my chapped lip. *Can her eyebrows reach up any further, I wonder?!* I bit back the hysterical laugh trying desperately to force its way out.

Nina was not done. Not by a long shot.

'So when you are back in this cloudy, damp Irish town, what *exactly* are you planning to do? Seeing as, and correct me if I'm wrong here, you don't know anyone, have no-one to call on, no starting point as to who this "girl" is, in fact nothing concrete to go on *at all*... Shall I continue?' She demanded, hands on hips, all pretence of washing up entirely abandoned. The still unwashed plates

3

stared forlornly back at me from where they were perched, haphazardly, next to the drainer.

'No, no, that's okay .. think you've about covered all the major points there.' I rushed out, deliberately keeping my back to her as I put the last clean plate into our cupboard, before making a quick, cowardly bolt for my bedroom.

In truth, Nina's words were worming their merry way into my already hesitant mind, after my somewhat extraordinary, and frankly insane, decision taken early this morning. I was bottling it, to put it bluntly. It actually felt quite comforting to feel this typical, normal reaction to anything new trying to barge its way in. My eyes fell upon my open suitcase with my neatly folded clothes, looking like rows of soldiers preparing for battle. I couldn't tell if they were praising or mocking this bold decision of mine.

I heard Nina come up behind, roughly wiping her hands on our checked tea towel, before throwing it in the vague direction of our kitchen. I literally itched to go pick it up and rehang it on our oven door.

Nina paused for a moment, taking in my betraying, shaking hands as I attempted to squeeze shut the case. Her small sigh filled the air. Then her hands reached down and covered mine, stilling me, before coaxing me to sit down beside her on the bed. Her pupils were large and fixed entirely on me. I fought against a strong urge to pull away. I really didn't want to hear her common sense words, particularly as it was usually me dishing out the sensible advice; not the other way round.

'Lily, my lovely lovely friend Lily. We've shared this flat, lived together for... my goodness, I don't know, for at least two years. I know I've always relied on you. You're the one who makes sure our bills are paid on time, there's always milk in the fridge, and all those other million things you do that I, shamefully, don't notice. And it's inspiring, really, I wish I could be like that. So this …this…' She paused, then threw up her hands, 'I'm actually at a lost for words and that, as you know, is truly staggering.'

A short reluctant laugh escaped me. Nina half smiled before grabbing my hands again, a little harder this time. 'So please, *please* tell me. Why are you really doing this? Are you in trouble? If you are-'

'No, no, I'm not,' I hastened to reassure her, 'At least, not in any physical or money kind of way.... though maybe within my mental state,' I mumbled too quietly for Nina to catch, shaking my head a little, as if hoping it would clear my buzzing mind. I forced myself to pull my thoughts together, to try and explain it as rationally as I could. 'I know how this looks, I know what I must sound like, believe me I do! I can feel my normal self trying to kick away this new, very irrational Lily.' I sat up straight now, my voice earnest and intent.

'But when I saw her, this woman, in my photo, when I would stake my very *life* on the fact she wasn't standing there the day I took it, something weird happened within me. It was like .. like she was calling me, pulling me towards her.'

My eyes were holding Nina's firmly now. My resolve and determination was strengthening with every word. 'I have to go.' I quietly confirmed, 'With complete and utter certainty, I know I have to go. She needs my help.'

My amber green eyes pleaded with her to understand. I knew how easy it was to still talk me out of this. Yet Nina's demeanour told me, very loudly, that she wasn't at all convinced by my argument. I couldn't blame her, not really.

She sighed again, gave a small despairing shrug of her shoulders, before finally letting go of my hands. I gave them a small discreet rub to ease back the circulation.

'Okay, if you feel that strongly, I guess you must go. But please, phone or text me as soon as you arrive so I know you're safe.' Her voice left no room for negotiation on this.

I smiled, a little in sheer relief, a little in trembling fear.

'I will. I promise.'

The room grew darker as day inevitably turned back to night. I now sat hunched over my laptop. My bulging suitcase was determinedly shut, waiting patiently by my bedroom door.

My eyes felt tired and itchy, but I still couldn't pull myself away from staring, and staring, at the photo in front of me - where this complete and utter madness had begun.

Inch Beach filled the screen with all its beautiful clear waters and warm flowing sand. Even though I was sitting miles away here in my dingy room, I felt its calmness and serenity reaching out and physically touching me. In the distance, I could just make out the emerald green rolling hills of Slieve Mountains, before the landscape dipped unseen into the Dingle Pennisular.

I'd travelled over to Ireland about six weeks ago, desperate for a short break, a change of pace from the relentlessness of my solicitor's office, where I worked as a legal secretary. My mum had once or twice mentioned Dingle in passing, though vague on the details of when we'd gone there as a family. Maybe it was nostalgia, maybe a stronger pull, but something had motivated me to book a flight to Kerry, then hire a car to drive to this fishing town.

And it was here, on this beach, on a quiet uneventful Wednesday morning that my heart had literally flipped over in joy as I stood on its calm, flat surface. The cold, driving rain, which seemed to have dogged me for the previous two days, had quietly drifted away, leaving a magnificent deep blue sky streaked with brushstrokes of white.

The tide was out; and it allowed the sky to perfectly reflect the beach below, creating this striking mirror image … to the point it was almost impossible to tell where the sky ended and sand begun. To me, on that day, standing there, it felt as if heaven itself had revealed herself in all her splendour and beauty and it had literally taken my breath away, in a way that rarely happened to me in the everyday.

For a while, absorbed in the here and now and not wanting to let this moment slip me by, I had pulled out my barely used compact digital camera my mum had given me a couple of Christmases ago, and began to snap away, finding I didn't actually need too much skill – the land was doing the framing for me. Then came this overwhelming urge to simply sit and take in the view before me, imprint it into my memory. I felt a peace drift over me like soft silk..... like I'd finally come home.

I was so reluctant to walk away that day, resisting until cold and hunger finally drove me off, and, in fact, in leaving Dingle itself the following day. Of course, while I'd been there I'd kept myself to myself, apart from chatting to my Bed and Breakfast lady, too shy as ever to introduce myself to any of the friendly locals. Yet, still, somehow I felt this strange "pulling back" sensation I'm so keenly feeling right now.

I'd tried to shrug this off, I really had. I fell back into my predictable job in our bustling Brighton office, sorted out the chaos Nina had left in the flat, phoned my mum, caught up with a couple of close friends. I know I would have carried on in this way, cosseted in my safe little world I'd so carefully constructed around me... had it not been for that photo.

They say, don't they, you can't fight your destiny, whoever "they" might be. But do we really, truly, believe that, here in the real world? I'm not sure. But I am having to accept that there are bigger things at play even I can't control.

It was quite a few weeks later when I had finally got round to downloading the photos from my camera onto my laptop. I felt excitement race through me as they began to flick up on my slideshow. Almost immediately I searched out, with breathless eagerness, the ones I'd taken that day on 'Inch beach'.

My eyes pounced immediately on it. Almost instantly, it was like being transported back to that very moment I pressed the shutter release button, knowing breathlessly, instinctively, that this would be the one I would frame for my bedroom wall.

But hang on…what's that black blot? Oh no, please don't tell me I had a scratch on the lens, or some sand stuck on it maybe.

Fighting a gut sinking feeling and holding my breath, I zoomed in onto the photo. The small dark form became a little larger. I continued to zoom again, and further again … until finally it took shape, became real. Became alive.

A sharp gasp escaped from me, my hand flying to my mouth in staggering shock.

For there, unnervingly clear on the enlarged photo, was a young woman's face – and she was staring directly at me. Her eyes were dark and compelling and there seemed to be an aura of … despair.. yes that was it ..despair surrounding her. Her hand seemed to be half raised towards me.

I couldn't tear my eyes away from her, though my mind was frantically trying to explain, apply some kind of reasonable logic. Perhaps I'd been mistaken? Perhaps I hadn't been alone that day after all? Maybe I just hadn't spotted her.

I quickly enlarged the other Inch Beach photos, to see if she appeared again, my eyes scan- burning them in a frantic rush. But no, all the others were as I remember - a deserted beach. A calm, serene 'giving no cause for alarm' image.

She drew me back to her. Of course she did. I was hooked, utterly hooked and couldn't look away.

'Why are you there?' I whispered out loud, my finger slowly stretching out to touch her as she stared back at me from the screen. 'Are you trying to ask me something? How on earth did I not see you?! I mean, are you even real? I don't get this... I really don't get any of this.'

I couldn't let it go, couldn't let *her* go. And I really tried to. But over the next couple of days she disturbed my dreams, my sleep, my conscious working day. It was like she wouldn't let me rest, or allow me to forget her. I had to do something, anything, before I drove myself mad with it.

So that's what I'm doing. Come tomorrow, as the restless night finally comes to an end, I'm going to board a plane back to Ireland and see where this craziness takes me. And if it takes me nowhere then no-one, except Nina, will ever know the embarrassing truth. Thank goodness.

My feet felt strange, leaden, as if there was a huge weight pulling them down, like sticky glue plastered all over my bare soles.

Confused, I looked down. I couldn't even see them properly; they were too covered in the wet sand, my toes curled deep within its sinking depths. My gaze slowly travelled down, as if seeing my body for the first time. I was wearing bright pink flower shorts. *My favourite,* I smiled in recognition. That's it! My mum had brought them for me when we first arrived here, unprepared as we were for the unseasonally warm May weather.

I froze, frowned, my young girl's mind perplexed, as I heard what I thought was the faintest sound of my name being called.

I looked around, yet couldn't see anyone. The wide stretch of sand suddenly seemed lonely, daunting. I became aware that my hand was clutching a plastic orange bucket decorated with colourful fish, splattered with sand, seaweed and what looked like a few broken shells.

'Lily! Lily where are you? We can't find you!'

I swung my head up at the demanding, exasperated voice, screwing my eyes up to try and spot in which direction it came from. The sun had peeped out from behind the cloud, dazzling me with its blazing glare. I blinked hard.

Then just as I was growing frustrated, annoyed even, three figures appeared as if from nowhere, scampering over the sand dunes. At first, they were small and faint, an unrecognisable dark mass, but then they began to take shape and turn into two unmistakeable boys of similar heights, and a smaller sized girl whose hair flew wildly around her.

'Oh at last! We've found you ...we thought you were never coming back to us!' I caught her words as they flew over to me in the gentle breeze.

I found myself smiling in delight and expectation, launching myself to run towards them.

But...wait...help... I'm stuck! I can't move!

9

My body began to shake and panic as I frantically tried to lift my feet. But the sand was sucking me down further, further, dragging my legs down now, then my hips, my torso... The piercing scream propelled itself out of me -

It took me several terrifying moments to realise I was sitting bolt right in my bed at home, that it had been my scream which had dragged me out of my nightmare.

My heartbeat was racing, my body sweaty, my duvet almost suffocating me within its tight hold.

Frantically kicking it away, I fell slowly back against the bed, closing my eyes, taking in deep shaky breaths to try and calm myself down.

What had that dream meant? They'd felt so real. Who were those children?

Who were they?!

Chapter Three

I gazed out of the miniature cabin window, as the plane began its final descent, unconsciously holding my breath until we had broken through the mass of suffocating cloud. A surprised smile lit up my face as I suddenly found myself blinded by a ray of sunshine bursting through the clouds, though it did force me to turn reluctantly away from the window.

Once the plane had finally landed and the usual craziness of everyone jumping up scrambling for bags and overhead luggage was over, I descended the metal stairs, stepping down onto the worn tarmac. We were guided across into Kerry's small airport terminal, the whiteness of the building glaring bright in the clear air. I couldn't resist stopping, closing my eyes for a moment, letting the unexpected warmth touch my face. It felt like a good omen and quite frankly I was happy to take that, as ridiculous as that may be.

Once through EU customs, which was fairly painless, I tracked down my car hire desk and before I knew it, was efficiently delivered to a Nissan Micra, an old fashioned paper map spread before me which was bearing all the hallmarks of constant use. I headed out onto the R561 Castlemaine road. My confidence grew as familiar sights popped up along the way, including a neglected roadside cafe I had stopped at last time, reassuring me that I was on the right route.

I felt shivers of excitement race through me as the moving scenery quickly became more impressive. I was dying to see Dingle Bay, and every once in a while it teased me with a glimpse of it. The bay nestled on the South West side of Ireland, with nothing but the wide open Atlantic Ocean beyond it, no land then in sight until the sea finally flowed onto American soil.

Just as the bumpy, potholed riddled road joined the N86 towards Dingle, I finally, *finally* caught a glimpse of Inch Beach. Without pausing to think, I pulled the wheel sharply over to the kerb; screeching the car to a shuddering stop. There was a loud, angry beep from the driver behind me, causing me a little twinge of guilt... but not for long, because I was too caught up in my eagerness to jump out of the door.

It was worth every worry, every anxious thought, every doubt over the last few days; to stand here now, the sun warming me while my eyes drunk in the view before me. Inch Beach, exactly as I remembered it, its stunning shape of a thumb stretching out from the main hand of Dingle itself. Its waters sparkled up to me, its deserted sand as smooth as cool marble.

I dared to peer ever more precariously over the rocky steep cliff edge; trying not to think about how high up I was. I smiled, laughed a little in delight, unexpected and welcome peace settling my slightly frayed nerves.

I stood for another precious moment. Took a mental photo. Breathed out. Then straightened up.

'Okay... okay. I'm ready.' I declared out loud to the birds gliding high and free above me.

With lighter feet, I returned to the car and happily drove the remaining few kilometres to the fishing town of Dingle itself, cranking up the scratchy radio to let the music blare out louder then I ever would have in England.

As I passed the town sign welcoming me to Dingle, I looked across to its bay, shaped in a perfect horseshoe. Many fishing boats of all sizes and conditions bobbed on the gentle lapping water, their mix of pristine whites to dirty browns, from bright red to dull greasy green. Shouts from fishermen mingled with the laughter and squeals of tourists hiring a charter for the day.

I turned into Strand Street and then Main Street, the heart of this small, proud fishing town. My eyes briefly touched on bustling shops targeting the tourists, to quiet tucked away bookshops rammed full of old dusty treasures. People were spilling out onto the road, the narrow pavements not coping with the demands put upon it by shopkeepers and pub owners sneakily leaking out from their establishments.

The road began a steep ascent and I encouraged the reluctant car, in the lowest gear I dared to use, to reach the top. We both sighed a breath of relief when we felt the road level off and I could turn left.

And there it is! I drove slowly into the car park, gazing up at the sign "Ciara's Bed and Breakfast" proudly emblazoned over the door of this pretty, yellow house that told you "Welcome!"

Ciara must have seen me pulling in, for the door flung wide open just as I was climbing out of the car. She stood, a smile lighting up her pretty face. I tucked a stray lock of brown hair behind my ear, breathed out, then walked up to her.

'Well now, when I saw your email a couple of days ago I couldn't believe it! Back so soon! Missing our emerald isle, were you now?'

I laughed, despite my nervousness, as her warm Irish lilt flowed like warm liquid over me. 'Something like that … and of course your lovely Irish breakfast.' I added with a touch of mischievousness.

Ciara grinned, encouraging me in. I could see her eyes were full of curiosity, but the polite hostess in her prevented her from giving voice to her questions bursting to get out. Which was not a bad thing right now, as I had no more understanding of what I was doing here then she did.

I discreetly looked at her as she insisted on taking my bag from me, wondering in almost awe and reverence as to how she kept so smart and elegant. *I mean, there is hardly a hair dislodged from its immaculate bob style, unlike my somewhat frizzy, and definitely thick unruly own. And how is it she's single; someone as stunning and easy going as her? Maybe this place doesn't give her time to pursue romance. Anyway, who am I to pass judgment, the original "spinster" girl herself?*

'Let's get you settled in. I thought you'd be liking the same room again.'

'Oh, that would be lovely, thank you.'

'And when you've unpacked, why don't you come down and find me for a cuppa… or maybe something a little stronger, if you catch my drift!'

I smiled, nodding. 'Thank you, I will.'

I made my way up the carpeted stairs, the iron key pressed tight into my hand.

It didn't take long to unpack my suitcase. I almost wished it had, for now I had no excuse in lingering within this safe haven. The room was tastefully decorated in pale peach, the wooden floor saved from being too cold by a beautiful large cream rug. I indulged my feet in its softness for a few blissful moments, before walking across to the bay windows. My bedroom was right at the top of the house, practically in the attic, and so offered me a fantastic view across the rooftops and chimney stacks to the distant harbour beyond.

After a few moments of absorbing, trying to empty my racing mind as I did, I turned away and sank down onto the soft bed.

Right, okay so I'm here... now what?

Mmmm, a good question. With no easy answer coming. *But don't panic yet.*

First thing to consider - can I trust Ciara? Confide in her? Will she think I'm totally insane... well of course she's going to! Let's face it, girl, you would too if the shoe was on the other foot.

But who else is going to know all the locals like she does? She might know this woman instantly! *Oh how incredible, amazing, would that be...*

And, anyway, what other options do I really have here, given I've only got the vaguest knowledge of the area, and some unreliable childhood memory I dreamed a couple of nights back; that may or may not be connected to all of this.

So come on Lily, stop sitting here, biting your already gnawed nails, talking to yourself like some nutter, trying to put off what you know you have to do. Pep talk over.

I drew in a deep shuddering breath.

Then slowly I stood up.

Chapter Four

I let out a guilty groan as the text flashed up on my phone screen, boldly displaying Nina's name. She had sent me a text yesterday and now, no doubt with mounting alarm at my rebuking lack of response, had resent it; only this time with bright exclamation marks all over it. It read "!!! *SO??????? Do I need to call 999?!!!*" . 'Please don't.' I muttered aloud as I fired back a quick "NO!! All fine thx in Dingle so don't call police! X" then, as a afterthought "ps don't forget to pay water bill!"

If only the second unanswered text in my inbox was as simple and straightforward to reply to. I felt my stomach clenching up as I stood there gnawing on my already bitten nail. Something had stopped me from calling her before I left for Dingle. Most likely because she was the one person in the whole world that had the power to undo my plans in an instant. Which was strange to admit to, because she had always been my greatest champion, the one who had been gently but firmly pushing me to try new experiences, broaden my horizon. But my mum was clearly worried about me. She had never been one to send lots of texts or call me unexpectedly; had always been happy till now to let me control the pace of our contact. Was it possible, somehow, someway, she knew something quite extraordinary had taken place within me? A mother's instinct maybe? I don't know, I'm not a mum .. yet, maybe never. This sudden thought depressed me for a moment.

I let out a long sigh, pausing to perch against a stony, not altogether comfortable wall that stretched out along the harbour side. For one still moment, I gazed out almost unseeing on the gentle bobbing boats drifting in the harbour, while my mind frantically tried to compose a far safer, yet cowardly text.

Sighing again without really realising it, I committed at last with a vague "Don't worry, I'm fine. Sorry should have called. I'm in

Dingle, trying to find a girl. Long story will explain ltr. Love you xxx". I quickly hit the send button before I re-agonised over it.

The text went zinging down its communication line. As Hannah Crossways's phone dutifully received it over 300 miles away, she quickly grabbed it then sat down heavily by her working desk. Relief flooded her face when she saw it was from her daughter 'At last!'.

That relief didn't last for long. Unbridled fear leapt into the same green eyes her daughter bore as she read on. Her palms grew sweaty, her face flushed. Her voice moaned softly. 'Dingle? Oh no! Why've you gone back? Why? My gorgeous girl whose never given me a moment's worry till now .... I've got to get her to come back, before she finds out-'

Without pausing or thinking it through, her mind frantic now with growing anxiety, Hannah pressed call against Lily's name. As the ringing tone filled the otherwise silent air, she silently pleaded for her daughter to pick up. *Please, please please..*

But the ringing continued on, relentlessly …

Back in Dingle, innocently unaware of the pandora's box I had opened, I switched my phone to silent mode, slipped it into my Cath Kidson spotty handbag, then continued walking up the steep path as I tried to find 'Café Peak'; proudly named after the Brandon Peak mountain range shadowing Dingle Bay.

Late into the night, Ciara and I had chatted through my so called "action" plan. Ciara had been surprisingly unfazed by my reason for coming back. If she thought I'd lost all sense and reason; she hid it remarkably well.

She had looked intently at the enlarged photo on my laptop, her forehead creasing deeply as she concentrated. I must confess I'd harboured a secret hope Ciara would be able to shed immediate light on who this was, and exclaim in true theatrical manner, 'But of course I know her!'

But of course she didn't. Ciara shook her head. 'Sorry, my lovely, I don't. She's never stayed here since I took over this place a couple of years ago, after moving down from Kilkenny. But she looks rather stunning, doesn't she?'

I had swallowed down hard on my disappointment, managing to nod in agreement as I took in the woman's long dark flowing hair and pale face. 'Yes, she does look beautiful... But how, what, and why is she in my darn photo, when I absolutely swear she wasn't there when I took it?!'

Ciara sat there in the cushioned leather sofa in her guest's lounge, the only ones still up at this late hour, shaking her head, nursing her Irish Coffee, clearly as flummoxed I was. Then, suddenly, her face had brightened, a mischievous glint appeared in her eyes. 'Oh, I do love a good mystery, don't you?'

When I raised my eyebrows sceptically, she had laughed good heartedly. It brought a warm smile to my face. Ciara had paused then, looked intently at me, then commented, 'You know, Lily, you should smile more. It lights up your face, brings out the green in those eyes of yours.' As I had felt a blush creep up over my cheeks, Ciara continued, 'In fact you have quite an Irish look about you with your brown curly hair, creamy complexion-'

'You mean pale complexion from lack of sun-'

'And with those eyes.' She gave a little shake. 'Perhaps your ancestors came from here. Certainly our folk like to branch out around the world, no mistaking that! It's the wanderlust in us.'

I grinned, took a sip of my own frothy warm Irish coffee Ciara had insisted I tried. It had left a delicious warm feeling through my body as it smoothed its way down, allowing my body to relax a little, give way.

After a moment, I finally dared to ask the question which had been burning to come out for ages. 'So… how do I find this girl, Ciara?'

'Well, that, my lovely, is the million euro question. I guess we should start with the obvious places like our 'friendly' police station, then around the local pubs – though I warn you there are a record breaking number of pubs here in Dingle – and just as many cafes, quite frankly. Use my name if you need to, I don't mind.'

'Oh thank you.' I gasped appreciatively, 'I have a feeling I may just need to do that...'

I had surprised myself by sleeping soundly, falling to sleep as soon as my head hit the silky pillow, then on waking be full of resolve and determination, something I frankly hadn't reckoned on.

Fuelled by this, and Ciara's very hearty breakfast, I set off on sneaker covered feet, calling in first at the local police constabulary, as it seemed the most obvious place to start.

I found myself inwardly cringing in anticipated embarrassment as I stepped through their ringing door, my deep flush creeping up my neck before I'd even made it up to the official looking desk.

A lone police officer; aged around fifty or so and hair tempered with grey, sat slouched over at the white plastic desk, flicking through what appeared to be a boating magazine. When he saw me, he quickly shoved it into the drawer below and plastered a professional smile into place. His face was tanned, lined, like he spent quite a few hours on his boat.

'Morning miss, how can I help you?'

'Uh ..hi. I'm hoping you can. I'm trying to track down someone. A woman. I think she lives around here.'

'Okay. Do you have a name, a last known address?'

I felt the flush reach my cheeks as I edged ever closer, pulling out my laptop from my flowery rucksack as I did.

'No.. just a photo. May I show you?'

He nodded his assent, but I could see he was already losing interest in my quest.

It was all so painfully slow waiting for my laptop to boot up, and locate the photo. By this stage he was barely holding onto his patience. The telltale crimson stain spread further up, till it reached the tips of my ears. I was back to gnawing my finger. *What on earth am I doing here, humiliating myself like this?!*

'Okay, I've found it.' I breathed out in relief, swivelling it round so he could see. As he leaned closer I caught sight of his name badge "PC Daryl Forster".

PC Forster gave it minimal due attention, before pushing out a tiny yet heavy sigh. 'I'm afraid I don't recognise her myself. But I've only been here for a few months,' he added 'I used to be stationed in Dublin.' He said this almost wistfully, yearning perhaps to be in that busy, vibrant city where he could be arresting real criminals, or at least drunk stag parties causing criminal damage in Temple Bar ... instead of being stuck here listening to some crazy fool of a girl.

He seemed then to remember his duty and tried to be helpful, perhaps brought on by a streak of genuine pity. Which was even worse. 'Have you asked around here? Though the locals are very tight knit.' He gave a wan smile. 'They sure know if there's a stranger amongst them.'

'I was planning to do that next. Are there any other avenues I can take? Anyone I can contact?' I knew I was grasping at straws before I'd even finished; PC Forster was already making grimacing expressions that was almost comical.

'Not really. Unless you want to get caught up in red tape, missing people bureaus and who knows what else, for quite frankly nothing to show at the end of it. If she's over eighteen, she can disappear all she likes and no one can do anything about it. Sorry, I know it's not what you want to hear.' This last bit was said almost apologetically. Almost.

It was also clearly a dismissal. I quickly stuffed my laptop away, gave an embarrassed smile, then practically ran out of there without even stopping to zip my bag up. I felt his eyes on me with every excruciating step.

Once outside I walked quickly down the street, trying to cool down my flaming cheeks. *"So that went well then"* my ironic side tried to joke.

'Well, you've lost all sense of dignity now ... might as well lose what remaining strands you still have.' I muttered to myself.

Bracing myself, I ducked into the first of many pubs along Dingle's two main streets...

Chapter Five

You would think in a small fishing town like Dingle it wouldn't take long to ask around at the local pubs … but no...

Ciara, it seemed, had been all too accurate in her prediction. I swear there were more pubs then houses here!

And each seemed to bear their own unique character and flavour, bursting with odd matched chairs and sticky tables, and too many people to be comfortably quiet. If I hadn't been so fraught with tension, I would have enjoyed taking in their different surroundings, delighted in taking pictures of the bizarre items I kept seeing adorning the walls, particularly the farming tools I spotted hanging precariously by nothing more than a very large and very rusty nail.

Dutifully I went around all of the locals and tourists lazily drinking as they idled the time away, their responses swinging from the barest shake of their heads before turning their attention back to their pints, to wanting to detain me in a "chat", their curiosity piqued. I inwardly sighed as once more I shoved my laptop away, once more drawing a very clear 'no' from the too busy and impatient pub owner. I had long ago cursed my stupidity for not printing out the darn photo after what felt like hours of my life wasted in waiting for the blasted laptop to boot up.

My enthusiasm, by now, had ebbed away as surely as my rubber soled shoes. Once outside, I reluctantly stared up the street. There was one pub left at the very end of the corner, proudly displaying the name "Smugglers". It seemed more modern and 'uncluttered' than the others.

Did I have the energy, desire or even the voice to ask the question, show her face once more? Or shall I just bail out until tomorrow. Or maybe the day after. Or the day after that. My throat was parched, my feet were sore, my head was starting to pound from lack of food and drink, and quite frankly all I could fantasise right now was laying on that beautiful, beautiful bed waiting for me at

Ciara's, clutching a restoring glass of anything. I didn't care what as long as it was cold.

I half turned to head back towards Ciara's. My feet had even been determinedly taking a step that way in anticipation.

Yet something propelled me to turn back once more and gaze at the "Smugglers". And then turn my whole reluctant self completely around and painfully walk towards it ... until I found myself standing in surprise outside its glazed wooden door.

And then I was inside, taking in, in almost a daze, its cool freshness and a smiling young man behind the bar encouraging me to approach. I let out a quick puff of breath and walked up to him, finding myself repeating my now familiar, 'I wonder if you could help me by taking a look at a photo of a woman I'm searching for?'

'Sure.'

'Thank you. I just need to boot the laptop up.'

I sensed him taking in my rosy cheeks, my not so discreet easing off of my shoes as I fell down onto the bar stool and the weariness clouding my eyes as I dragged my reluctant laptop out of its case.

'How about I pour you a nice cold one while you wait for that to boot up? You look like you might need it.'

I closed my eyes for a blissful moment and sighed out. 'Oh yes please. But better make it of the non alcoholic variety or I'll crash out asleep right here on your bar.' I reluctantly added.

He grinned, held out his hand. 'The name's Greg. New to these parts, aren't you? That I know because no-one round here ever plumps for the soft kind of drink!'

I found myself smiling back as I reached out my hand to accept his. 'Its Lily. Yes, kind of. Did a fleeting visit a month or so back. Now I'm back to ... kind of solve a mystery.'

Greg nodded towards my laptop as it made its painful process of powering up, as if it too was exhausted by its efforts. 'So there's a picture of a lady you want to show me?'

'Uh .. yes. I know, I know its sounds crazy, you don't need to tell me.' I rushed on.

He merely shrugged, smiled again as he expertly opened up a lemonade bottle for me, then poured it into a frosted glass. 'Well you are in Ireland. You have to be a little crazy, it helps, trust me on that.' He put the drink down in front of me, giving the bar counter a quick flick of his cloth as he did so.

I found myself relaxing as I nearly drowned half the glass, discreetly quieting a burp from erupting. I could see Greg biting back a laugh, and avoided looking up for a moment.

'Okay... I've got the picture up.'

'Let's be having a look then.'

I turned the laptop round and Greg closed in to have a look. A small frown appeared almost immediately. I found myself catching my breath in anticipation.

'She does look familiar.'

'She does?!' I cut in excitedly, before straining to rein it back in. He continued to stare at the grainy photo. You could see his mind trying to shift through a catalogue of faces filed away.

'Yeah, she really looks like an old mate of mine. But I don't know, its hard to see her face clearly and anyway my mate had short, blond hair, skinny as anything and wore scary gothic make-up...' His voice trailed off.

Please, please please... I began to feverishly pray, *have a name for me.*

'Ah...your computer's seems to have closed the program down.' Greg spun my laptop round to show me. There was only the desktop icon page blinking slowly at me. I groaned, very loudly, and uttered an unladylike oath.

'Sorry, sorry.' I rushed out, 'just let me-'

'Oh listen, leave it for a minute, give your computer a well deserved break. To be honest, I might be leading you up a false path. Anyways, I moved away after finishing college, and only found my way back here a couple of years ago, so not sure I can help any further. I'm pretty crap at recognising people standing right in front of me.'

I tried to smile, though feared it was more of a grimace. 'I think you're just saying that to be kind. But okay, I'll give in for now. Thanks anyway for looking.' I made to move, shutting the stubborn laptop down as I did.

'You know, it might be worth asking David. He runs "Cafe Peak", just up the road. He's lived here forever and a good mate of mine. Tell him I sent you.'

Greg was giving me an encouraging smile, perhaps sensing my sudden reluctance to ask another stranger who no doubt would look at me oddly then send me on my way with my tail between my legs, my posture stooped ever downwards.

'Really? You really think so?'

'Yes, I do! Don't give up yet, not yet.'

Something about him; whether it was the earnestness of his voice, or the determination in his eyes as they looked at mine, jolted me enough to find myself nodding in agreement. I would do this last call, even though every fibre in my body wanted to crawl back to the safe haven of Ciara's, and sleep and sleep before flying my way back home under the blissful cover of darkness...

'Hey, make sure you come back now for a drink. Don't go disappearing without saying goodbye.'

Was he a mindreader?!! I spun round from the doorway and found myself giving a short laugh and a nod, my smile widened while thinking *were you sent to stop me giving up on this?* Then I gave myself a big mental shake, *stop getting so fanciful, for goodness sake.*

And so that's how I found myself standing outside a equally tastefully looking 'Cafe Peak'. It boasted nice large wooden windows that could be opened out to allow the freshness in when the weather was warm, as it was today with the summer scented air gently blowing around us. A few table and chairs were carefully positioned to maximise the views of the harbour below from where the cafe stood at the top of a rocky path. At one of them, a young couple, who looked like they had stepped out of a magazine, sat drinking their steaming chocolate sprinkled grande coffees, holding hands and chatting easily. I felt a strange, unfamiliar feeling as I quietly passed them by, and slowly realised, to my shock, that it must be envy. I shook my head, totally flummoxed by my irrational reaction. But still unsettling thoughts persisted in jolting me. *What must it feel like to be so comfortable and at ease with another, where they intimately know your innermost longings, and desires, your fear and insecurities? Is it so powerful you can't fight it, or even want to? Or does it fill you with deep deep fear to know they could so easily, if they chose to, destroy your trust and faith in them?* I forced the thoughts away, giving myself a ticking off.

The cafe was alive with chatter, laughter and whistling steam coffee as I pushed open the door, despite the lateness of the hour. The deco was as tasteful inside, with the same warm tones of brown and cream, the walls spared from being empty by photos of the local areas, mostly done in sepia. I found my eyes drawn to them as soon as I had stepped in.

I approached the counter where two people stood serving. One was a young girl, her blond hair boldly streaked with pink, no older then twenty, smiling as she served a customer. The other, who must be David, stood at the coffee machine coaxing it into producing great froths of steam.

He looked up over the steam, as if he sensed my intensive eyes on him. Blue grey eyes met mine and as they did, I felt something odd happen within me, like my heart had taken a sudden faster beat. Surprised at my reaction, I took a step back, then tried to cover this as he gave me a friendly but polite smile.

'Afternoon, what can I get you?' His warm Irish tones enquired.

I gave myself a mental shake, trying to get back some sense of normal behaviour. Yet something about that voice and eyes.. it was if they were familiar to my alert senses. Which was frankly just impossible.

Aware he was beginning to look at me oddly, I cleared my voice and tried to speak up over the din of the machine. 'Oh um, just a latte please.'

As he nodded, starting to crank the machine up again, I spoke again while my nerve held.

'Your friend, Greg, sent me to you-'

He paused, grinned properly for the first time. 'Did he now? Well, he knows his limits, and between you and me,' He leaned a little closer, nearly scalding himself in the process, 'coffee at his bar is .. wait for this you may be shocked ...instant! Instant - imagine the shame of that!'

'Imagine.' I faintly repeated. As he went back to the machine, chuckling to himself, I tried again, 'Anyway, the thing is-'

'Do you want skimmed or semi with that? I know what you ladies are like always watching the waistline. Not that I'm suggesting you need to, of course.'

I stared at him as he smiled blandly again, flummoxed as to whether he was being polite, charming or downright rude.

'Semi is fine. As I was saying-'

'Double or single espresso? Need a little muffin with that? Baked this morning by my own fair hands.'

'Ah, no, no thanks. And just a single.' I rushed on before he could ask me any more inane questions, though couldn't help admiring his polished selling technique. 'The thing is, I'm looking for someone and I wondered if I could show you her photo. Greg thought you might know her.'

He looked up, a little surprised by my request. 'Well, sure now I can have a look.'

As I went to get my laptop out, his hand reached out to stop me. The unexpected touch against mine felt a little too intimate, confusing ... but did make me pause.

'Why don't you go take a seat over there?' He pointed to a nearby empty table. 'I'll bring your coffee over, then you can show me.'

I found myself obediently doing his bidding. I felt oddly warm inside, flushed, and still couldn't shake that deja vu feeling we had met before.

Several minutes passed, giving me time to power up the tired old laptop, gaze around and try to compose my somewhat turbulent thoughts.

'Sorry about the wait. No rest for the coffee makers of this world.'

I turned from looking at an aerial photo of the peaks; capturing beautifully the rawness of the mountain, to find myself with company. There before me sat my frothy chocolate coated latte, complete with an accompanying miniature biscuit and a bowl of sugar. It looked almost too perfect to drink.

'So I'm David, but I'm guessing you know that already.' David smiled at me, leaning back on his chair. His black hair was a little wild, as if he spent the whole time raking it off his forehead.

'Yes. I'm Lily. I'm staying at Ciara's. Do you know her?' I knew I was gabbling, stalling him when he probably needed to go back to serving, but I found I couldn't stop the words from spurting out. *I know I'm going to be feel embarrassed about this later, I can just feel it.*

'I do. Best breakfast in town.'

'That's what I tell her!'

We shared a smile. All at once he was looking at me intently, as if I was a riddle to be solved. I felt my betraying flush seeping in. 'Excuse me for asking, but have you stayed round here before?'

'I did recently, but only for a couple of days. I think I came here as a kid with my mum.' *Why am I telling you all this?*

I became aware that a little queue was forming at the counter and his assistant was trying to catch David's eye. David motioned to her 'one minute!'. I sensed I was losing his concentration, as his fingers started tapping the table and he slightly raised himself off the chair in preparation to fly back to the counter.

'Sorry, I have to get back before Dora resigns on me.'

'Of course, sorry! Let me show you quickly.'

He resat down and our heads came close together as I quickly spun the laptop around so he could take a look.

David eyes moved down to look at the photo, no doubt to humour me. I already started imagining in the next moment he would look up, shake his head apologetically as so many had before him, smile as he stood up, encourage me to have a muffin after all, before returning to what appeared to be a nice, safe and easy life in this cafe he probably had built up from nothing... And most certainly forgetting me in the next breath.

But life doesn't always follow what it should. It doesn't always give you the easy route. Sometimes we have to go down the difficult winding path, covered in sharp stones, to find the answers to our searching. We can't shut ourselves off forever, believing if we don't think or feel or love or discover the truth, we can just carry on existing. Just like I had been, until I stepped onto that plane yesterday.

And unbeknown to me, David carried pain and heartache so acutely and deeply inside him he had learned to live with it, creating instead this carefree persona I was witnessing today. In this moment, in this suspended moment, I didn't know any of this, didn't know what I was about to inflict on him. If I had, would I still have done this; begun this spiralling chain of events?

As we sat now at his cafe table, a slow dawning realisation came over me that all was not right. This was quickly followed by complete horror as I saw his face drain away, the smile slip off, his whole body freeze as he stared and stared at the photo. It was like his very essence had been pulled out of him, leaving behind only a barely breathing man.

'What is it?' I finally dared to whisper.

His eyes slowly lifted and I found myself gasping as they clashed with mine. They were dark with pain and distress and I found my hand reaching out to his, aghast I had done this; triggered something so terrible within him.

As I did though, it was like a ball of fury took over him. He slammed the laptop shut, narrowly missing my fingers, causing a couple of people to turn round. His hand then grabbed mine in a vicelike grip that nearly made me cry out.

'What kind of sick joke is this?! Why do you have this photo?!'

'I , I 'm sorry I don't-'

'Tell me, who are you?! Tell me!'

I tried to break in, stutter something but he was relentless in his anger. Everyone had stilled around us, staring openly now.

From over at the counter, Dora was trying to act normal. But obvious shock was spilling out of her at witnessing this complete out of character reaction from her boss.

David abruptly flung my hand away, rising. As he did the chair fell back, banging loudly as it hit the floor, charging the air around it. I could only stupidly stare, shaking my head in bewilderment, naively unprepared to salvage this. *Oh God please tell me, what have I done?!*

He leaned closer again, closing his eyes, his breath heavy and laboured as he fought hard to control himself. When his eyes did fly open, the sparks still flew at me though his voice held an unnatural controlled tone that somehow unnerved me more. The words were forced out from between his clenched jaw.

'Why the hell are you looking for my sister?'

Chapter Six

His stare was hard, his breath rapid. His hands, where they gripped the table, were clenched white.

I stared back at him, my brain trying to react, think, say something. *Anything*! I was all too acutely aware of the hushed silence now descended over the cafe, and the burning hot feel of eyes on us.

David pushed back from the table so forcefully it began to wobble in a dangerous way. My creamy coffee couldn't fight against it and toppled over, forming a large staining puddle across the glossed table wood. Instinct kicking in, I grabbed my laptop just in time. As I did, it began to dawn on my befuddled mind that David was walking out, pushing roughly past everyone as he did, clearly desperate to get out of there … and away from me.

'David?! Where are you going?!' It was Dora, her voice full of alarm as she stared bewildered after him.

It was enough to spur me into action. Frantically I grabbed my bag, cramming the laptop into it whilst I dashed after him.

I saw him as I fell out onto the pavement. He was walking fast, cutting a distraught figure, his fists still clenched tight by his sides.

'Wait, please! David, wait!' Almost colliding into him in my haste, I flung myself in front of his pathway, stretching out a pleading hand. 'Please, let me explain-'

His hands suddenly gripped my arms, his fingers cutting deep into my blood flow. I bit back a shocked cry.

'Explain?! You think you can explain this?! You don't get it, you damn fool of a girl!'

Anger seeped out from every pore of him and I hated this feeling of … fear… and the humiliating tears now brimming my eyes; evidence of a weakness where I yearned to be strong and unaffected. 'Please, let go of me.' I cried out. 'You're hurting me!'

I felt the pressure of his punishing fingers for another intense moment; then they were gone. David was stepping back, giving a low moan, his hands pushing wildly through his distressed hair. 'What am I doing?' I caught the words as the wind all at once picked up and whirled around us.

I took a deep breath, allowing us a much needed moment, then dared to move a little closer to him. I mustered up every ounce of confidence I could scrap together.

'Let's sit down here. Let me explain it all to you, and maybe we can work this out.. together.' He turned sharply and stared at me. 'Please.' I urged.

I sat down on the wall, willing him to follow, and after a long conflicting moment, he did. His leg moved restlessly up and down and he refused to meet my eyes. But at least he seemed a little calmer.

'I know me coming here like this is a complete shock, I can see that. You don't know who I am and this photo of .. your sister?' I hesitated to get confirmation. With evident reluctance he gave a short nod of his head, swallowing. 'I can see its causing you distress. I'm sorry, it wasn't my intention.' I paused, then dared to say, 'Can I tell you how I came to have this photo?'

Silence greeted my request, so I stumbled on, cursing the inadequacy of words alone at my disposal. 'I was on holiday here in Dingle – I think I already told you that, sorry – and when I got home and looked at my photos, on this particular photo was a woman ... your sister ... But you see I *know* I was alone on the beach that day-'

I broke off as David stood, agitation pouring out of every pore. He was staring down at me in disbelief. 'You expect me to believe this load of crap?! That my sister, *my sister* who I haven't seen or heard one word from in over five years, appeared like… like… some magic trick on your photo and you decided to just drop whatever it was you were doing … *to find her?* Is this the best you can come up with?! Do you take me for some Irish dunce of a fool, huh?!'

He was towering over me again. It was unnerving, daunting, and put me at a disadvantage. I hastily jumped to my feet, trying to engage his eyes with mine to...I don't know!... show him my sincerity or something.

'Yes, that's my story! And believe me I know how it sounds! I know I sound like a nutcase. But she appeared to me and I had to respond.... *Why would I make this up*?!'

'I don't know! I don't know! I don't know who or what you are!'

We both paused in our own turmoil. David was pacing back and forth, as if he couldn't allow himself to be still.

He finally turned back to me. I stared at him, tense, waiting, my nerves wound tight, an ominous feeling descending over me that I couldn't shake off. *Oh no...*

'Alright then, if you think she is "calling" to you, " his hands sarcastically made speech marks, I flinched. 'then prove this to me. We'll go back to this beach right now and you can take a photo with this supposed magical camera of yours and if she appears again on your photo then I will believe this crappy yarn of yours. If not, I'm escorting you in person to our local constabulary and they can deal with you.' His eyes were hard, unforgiving. And challenging.

'Actually we've already met.' I found myself muttering, feeling a rise of hysteria building within me again.

'Well, that's grand then, isn't it. Wont need to make any introductions.'

His voice was flippant, sarcastic. But if you listened a little closer, you could hear the faintest note of desperate hope. And that power undid me in a second.

Why am I even contemplating this? I know to even entertain this crazy plan would only drag us both into disappointment ...and for me complete and utter humiliation on every level possible.

But what could I do?! I couldn't let go now, I'd come too far. It had me in its grip, despite my every rational misgiving.

As I stood alone on that sudden cold blustery spot of Dingle, the wind buffering me from every side, as did the equally cold stare of a man who was a stranger; yet wasn't, I found myself muttering up a silent plea of help to whoever was listening. And then something rather extraordinary and weird happened to me.

An unexpected smile broke out across my face, and it took us both back. 'Okay,' I nodded, 'let's go then.'

The rigid shock on his face was priceless, and almost worth my inevitable demise to come.

We had been mute with each other, two strangers thrown together, as we drove in David's blue sedan car over to Inch Beach. The fifteen minutes seemed to be the longest minutes of my life and my nails suffered badly.

With relief, I saw the brown tourist sign for the beach before us, and so desperate was I to get out of the confined space, I literally jumped out before he had even turned the ignition off. I think at this point I no longer cared if this worked or not. I just wanted to get this over with.

Amazing myself when considering these fraught circumstances, I lead David straight to the exact spot, every step of mine matched by his own dominating one. His fury had now turned to stony silence and, without doubt, mixed in with a huge chunk of resentment at my unwanted interference in his family. I could feel his defences sending out sharp signals to keep my distance. I was all too happy to comply.

I pulled out my innocent yet guilty camera and tried to work out precisely which angle I had been standing in when I took the photo. *Though does it really matter?* Came the humourless thought. Once again the beach was deserted of strolling walkers or barking dogs racing in and out of the moving waves, and once again, despite everything going on, I was struck anew by the sheer beauty of this stretch of sand.

After I took a calculated guess and taken a couple of shots, I shoved the camera away, breathed out a deep shuddering breath I had unconsciously been holding, then slowly turned to my silent companion as he looked unseeing across the horizon.

His thoughts appeared oppressive, weighing him down and I felt a weird intense desire to ease them away somehow ... out of sympathy or because I was the cause of them, I didn't know and that left me feeling confused. I swallowed, hard, then found my voice.

'We'll need to head to Ciara's where I'm staying to download them.'

'Sure, sure. Let's carry on this jolly little field trip.' His tone was condescending, belittling as he swept his hand out in a some kind of pretend act of chivalry.

At this, a sudden unexpected spark of anger flared up within me, an emotion I rarely felt. My eyes flashed at him. He caught them full on (how could he not?) and to my surprise, choked back down what verbal insult he was about to throw next at me.

We made our way back to the car at a fast pace despite the sinking sand, both keen to get this over and done with. David drove without asking for instructions to Ciara's place. I let us in with the key entrusted to me. A tremendous feeling of relief swept through me to find it empty, its air still, as if it too was holding its breath.

As I set up the computer I felt his large presence intimidate me. The room felt small. Far too small. I waved a vague hand towards the tea tray across the room in some vain hope he'd walk across and make us a drink, thereby giving me some much needed breathing space. But I couldn't resist adding, with a sarcastic bite to my tone. 'I would suggest you go get a drink from downstairs, but I don't want to be accused of using some photographers tricks on the photo.'

David narrowed his eyes. 'So thoughtful of you,' came the moody reply. However, he did as bidden and walked over to the tray. I closed my eyes for a moment, before self consciously tucking some curls behind my ear in an attempt to tidy it after the wind had whipped it up good. Probably an inappropriate moment to be worrying about how I looked – *and just where had that desire to look nice come from...*

With all of this whirring around me, my hands felt sweaty and uncoordinated as I started to download the photos. My pulse quickened as the images from today started to rapidly appear. I searched for the particular one we wanted. I felt David's breath on my neck from where he had silently come up behind me.

I double clicked on it, held my breath. David leaned closer still.

This time I did not even have to zoom in to see her face. It was clear, brazenly clear.

His staggered gasp filled the air. The hot sugared tea in his hand fell unnoticed to the floor, staining forever the soft cream rug beneath. Air and time seemed to freeze around us, as if capturing us in its picture frame.

There had been a beginning to this, and I'd taken the first step. But now it wasn't just about me and a stranger's face; it was time for him to come and walk this with me, to search for the truth.

Our reasons for doing this – for him to find his missing sister, mine to discover why she had appeared to me - were very, very different …but our destination would be the same.

It was much later. We were vaguely aware of the light slowly fading away as we sat outside David's cafe, nursing our almost cold coffees. He had closed up a while back, acting mostly on autopilot, though his apology to Dora was, without doubt, sincere in leaving her in the lurch like that.

I took it as a good sign of his strength and character that, although clearly annoyed with him, she accepted his apology gracefully and even laughingly promised that yes she would be back in the morning ... though a little overdue pay rise may be in order.

A shift had taken place within our 'relationship'. David's eyes no longer blazed in anger and resentment towards me. And for that I was very grateful - no one wants to be the enemy.

But still he was wary of me. I keep catching him giving me narrow sidelong looks, his eyes trying to assess me. And who could blame him really? I would be too, if our roles were swapped.

Now all I could think of was this huge, burning provoking question searing away at me - how do I get him to open up about his sister? Mm exactly. Not an easy one. Maybe for the moment I'll keep to safer topics.

'It's so peaceful here, I can see why you like it.' I gazed down at the harbour. 'I should have brought my camera.' I turned to look at David, to show him the soft teasing in my eyes.

David arched his eyebrows but I could see the twitching of his mouth as he fought back a smile. 'To be honest I'm not sure I've bonded too well with that camera of yours.'

I laughed in unexpected delight. It felt *so* good after the stress of the day. My laugh must have been infectious; for a full smile spread slowly across David's face, softening his eyes. I inhaled in surprise, taken aback.

We smiled at each other for another moment, holding the gaze. Then a little awkwardness hurried back, as if it needed to remind us of why we were thrown together like this in the first place.

We turned away, both mutely looking down at the drinks cradled in our hands.

After a long painful silence, I could stand it no more.

'So...'

'So.' He echoed, half turning his head towards me. 'I guess you want to know about my sister.'

Taking my silence as affirmation, David continued, 'Her name is Natalie.. Nat, as we all call her.' His voice was a little raspy, raw, as if saying her name out loud was almost too much. 'She looked a lot different last time I saw her; much shorter hair, blonde not dark like it is now in your photo, a little lighter in weight. But I would still know her anywhere.'

No wonder none of the locals recognised her when I showed them this photo. And that explains Greg's confusion. It was starting to make sense now, when you consider how small a community it is here and how everyone seems to knows everyone.

I nodded as these thoughts whirled around my head, gently encouraged him on. 'Go on.'

'We grew up here in Dingle. My mum still lives here. My dad .. well he passed away a couple of years back now, from cancer.' David swallowed, hard. 'Nat doesn't even know.' His voice broke. His face turned away. I felt his pain and had to swallow hard to stop

35

unexpected tears. I instinctively reached out my hand, gently covering his, wanting to offer some kind of comfort. He didn't pull away from my touch, so I kept it there. His words began to flow a little easier then.

'You know we were just an average family growing up here. I don't know to this day what happened, when everything just started to unravel. Mam and Pa had been fighting, but of what who knows; Mam never talks about it. Nat and I had always been close, she used to hang out with me and my mate Sean, then with Amy, Sean's wife, after they got hitched. Looking back now, I can see Nat slowly withdrew from us sometime after that. Stopped coming out with us, no longer came to me for advice, that sort of thing, you know? I felt it, but didn't know what to do. I was starting up this cafe then and living in the flat above, so didn't go home as much. Believe me, I kick myself, ask myself over and over if I could have done something to stop her leaving.'

David's eyes were anguished as he turned to me, shaking his head. 'You never think something like this will happen to you, that one ordinary day you mam will phone you, crying so hysterically you can barely understand her, telling you your baby sister has disappeared leaving us nothing but some scrawled goodbye message telling us "not to worry"'. His voice had risen an octave in his agitation. 'Not to worry?! Was she out of her friggin mind! How could we do anything but?!'

I leaned closer still, grasped his hand now. Gave him a moment. All the while my mind was trying to break down what he had told me, to make some sense of it.

'So this note was all she left for you?'

He gave a humourless laugh. 'Yep, that's all she left us.'

'And you tried to .. find her?' I asked, not thinking it through.

I knew instantly it was the wrong thing to say. I cringed as David's outrageous eyes flew to mine, my hand pushed angrily away. 'What do you take me for?! Some insensitive selfish brute who didn't give a damn his sister had disappeared to who knows where?! Of course I looked for her, but do you know how impossible it is to find someone who doesn't want to be found?'

I did, I wanted to say, or at least I'm beginning to. But he was standing up now, glaring at me, his voice dripping with sarcasm as he yanked away my cup. 'Well, thanks for this chat. Like to say it's been grand, but that would be a lie. Enjoy messing with someone else's life.'

That got to me. I suddenly felt insanely and uncharacteristically angry. I moved round the table and yanked on his arm hard enough to stop him from taking any more than a couple of steps away.

'Would you just quit huffing off every five minutes like... like some sulky little boy! For crying out loud!' I closed my eyes for a moment, aware of his eyes casting daggers into me. I grabbed his other arm to stop any attempt to push me aside, slamming down my cup he'd been holding on to.

'Look, you don't have to like me. I know I'm not the easiest person to like. Though quite frankly, neither are you!' I muttered darkly, steely eyes locking with his. 'But for whatever reason I've yet to fathom your sister came to me, to *me*, and it was a cry for help in the most unusual and immense way. I'm not going anywhere until we discover where she is, I'm not turning my back on her now. So this is what is going to happen. You and me are going to work together and you are going to accept that and stop fighting me on this. Please.' I added, a little breathless from my rant.

I found myself watching his chest rise and fall rapidly as he fought an internal battle over me. Then, in breathless wonder I watched a slow acceptance come over him. His breath slowed to a normal pace, his body unwound a little.

'Always this fiery in nature?' Came his reply at last, giving me a long look.

I bit back a shocked laugh, a little staggered. 'Would you believe me if I said that no-one has ever accused me of being fiery before?' I managed to stumble out.

His eyebrows shot up. His head cocked thoughtfully to one side. 'Then I guess you've never cared this passionately about something before.'

I stared at him, at his startling revelation of his words. Was that true? Have I lived my life so carefully, so much in the safe lane I've never once allowed this side of my nature to come fully to life before? *Oh my goodness... he's right. How can that be?*

I was aware that David was looking intently at me, a surprised expression touching his features.

Our eyes held for a moment. Then we broke away. David gave a small cough, then nodded pointedly to my hands which still gripped his arms. 'I think you can probably let go of me now... before I have permanent bruises on my arms.'

I narrowed my eyes. 'You're not going to run away?'

An infectious laugh escaped through his lips. 'No, I'm not going to run away, for the love of all things!'

I nodded, then let him go.

'You know, I think I need a pint of the good stuff. Come on, fiery.'

We walked along the road towards the now familiar "Smugglers" pub. As we did, I was struck by a sudden thought. I stopped dead in my tracks, taking David a moment to realise. When he did, he paused, turned to me. 'Come on, that pint is growing warmer as we speak.'

'Sorry. I was just thinking. When did Nat disappear, precisely? I know it was five years ago, but what date exactly?'

'June twentieth. That date is kind of etched on my mind, as you can imagine.'

I gasped. 'Oh my goodness David, that's exactly the date I was here when I took that original photo! That can't be a coincidence, can it?'

David stared at me for the longest time. 'No … no it can't,' he finally breathed out.

Chapter Seven

'Ah, so you found each other.' The voice bellowed out at us as soon as we shut the glazed door behind us.

Greg appeared to be standing in almost the same spot as earlier, with that ever permanent towel slung over his shoulder, and his hands doing it continual filling of sparkling glasses. He grinned broadly at us.

'Yeah, remind me to "thank" you for that later.' David commented wryly as we walked across to him.

I chose to rise above this barbed comment and instead focus on the easy going and, quite frankly, less intense Greg, who right then felt like a most soothing balm to my somewhat frayed self.

'Hi Greg.' I smiled warmly, taking even me by surprise. Greg seemed equally taken aback by this, but came right back at me with one of his own. David frowned, looking from one to the other of us, a direct questioning look in his eye.

Being the ever professional barman, Greg quickly drew David in as he deftly handed a nearby punter his drink. Without pausing, he started pouring one for David without enquiring what his tipple would be. To me he asked, 'Another long cold one? Maybe a touch of alcohol in it this time?'

I nodded eagerly. 'Yes please.'

Greg turned to David. 'When this young lady came into my pub earlier today, seeing if I knew the girl in her photo,' He turned to me, with an almost apologetic smile 'to be sure if she didn't need one very large cold drink; her cheeks were that red!'

I could feel that same telltale red flush erupting now as the two men both turned to study my "infamous" cheeks.

'I think I recognised her, the girl, but the picture was quite grainy,' Greg continued on. I felt David's body tense beside me. 'Thought you might be the best person to ask, Dave. Do you know her?' He looked now with interest at David.

Such a simple innocent question. Such an impossible complex question.

'Uh..' David stuttered, struggling to know how to answer Greg without opening up too many probing questions. As far as everyone in the community was concerned, including Greg, Natalie had moved away and rarely had time to visit. David and his mum had successfully hidden the more god awful truth - that she had in fact simply "disappeared". And I wasn't going to be the one to break this silence after five long years.

'No, not really, just like you.' I fibbed, cutting in. I rushed on, giving neither the chance to react. 'But it seems I've met two helpful chaps here in Dingle, because David is going to try to help me as well. Great, eh?' With that I offered up a smile, along with a 10 euro note, then grabbed my cold glass of rose wine put down in front of me. 'Shall we sit over there?' I suggested without waiting for a reply, my desire to escape into a dark corner overwhelming me. I scooted over to a tucked away table I had spied earlier.

David slid into the chair opposite, a pint placed in front of him. His hand covered my busy one as it fussed with the beer mats. I looked up. There was warmth and appreciation in his eyes. 'Thanks.. you know for not-'

'It's okay. You can trust me with this.' I urged, wanting him to understand. It felt so important right then for him to believe in me, lean on me a little. 'I'm not going to start announcing the truth to anyone.'

There was an intense moment as he weighed up my words. I held his challenging gaze as steadily as I could. Finally, satisfied, he nodded, leaned back a little as he let go of my hand to reach for his beer. The tension evaporated away like fine mist. I felt my shoulders drop in relief.

After we had both taken some refreshing sips, I opened my mouth to broach the subject that we both knew we had to confront – where do we go, what we should do next in finding Natalie?

David, it appeared, had other ideas. He was leaning back into his seat, putting one slightly muddy boot against the table edge. This image just didn't seem to fit in with the man I had spent excruciating hours with today and flew me right off course. I realised I was still sitting there with my mouth agape like some gasping goldfish. I snapped my lips shut.

'So I feel we're not of an equal standing here, Lily.'

Okay, not sure I'm liking this. I frowned, an uncomfortable sensation growing in the pit of my stomach. 'What do you mean?' I asked suspiciously.

'Well, since you came bursting into my life approximately-' He looked at his watch and did a mental count, 'five hours ago or thereabouts,' *Was it only that long?* 'I feel I've revealed rather a lot of me... and not all of it good.' At this, he looked almost embarrassed. 'Yet now it seems you know things, real deep personal things, I've had no intention of telling anyone, least of all some girl who has just walked off the street and into my cafe.'

David leaned forward, his arms bracing the table as he locked me with his stare. 'Yet here you are... and now you do. So forgive me for feeling like its time the attention shifted onto you for a few minutes.'

How could anything about me possibly be of interest to someone like you?

'I can, but I'm not really that exciting. That is, my life isn't.' I stammered out, half apologetically. I suddenly felt nervous and .. exposed, as his scrutinising eyes refused me the mercy of looking away. I gave in, but ungraciously. 'What do you want to know?'

He half smiled at that. 'Well, you know the usual kind of things. Where you live, what you do, your full name ... I'm sure you get the idea. Would have drawn you up a questionnaire if I had known you were arriving.'

'Oh ha ha.' I muttered darkly as he amused himself at my expense. 'Okay fine, but at least I've warned you its pretty boring. I live in Brighton in Sussex, on the coast,' I added, 'Famous for its lanes, the pier, stag and hen dos, Graham Greene's 'Brighton Rock-"

'Been there actually, but thanks for the quick whistlestop tour.'

'Okay! Just trying to make this a little more exciting for you here!' I saw his eyes narrow at that, as if he could see right through my

41

flippancy to see the truth buried painfully deep inside me... that sometimes I wondered what value I brought to the world I existed in.

'I work for a solicitors office; and I really wont bore you with the finer details of what we do, especially as I've probably been sacked anyway for taking unplanned leave. Which if anyone who knew me would tell you would normally send me into a complete breakdown.' I rambled on, aware and staggered that instead of being bored by me, David was still listening, his eyes fixed unwavering on me. *What was he thinking? Maybe it's a blessing I don't know.* 'My mum lives nearby. My Dad passed away a little while back, so its just me and my mum. I live with Nina, who is lovely but completely hopeless with paying bills so no doubt, as well as going back to no job, my flat will be in complete darkness and there'll be no running water!'

I was attempting to be funny, but in saying those words out loud I began to feel a small panic that there may be more than an ounce of truth in them. Maybe I should call her, just to make sure...

David, meanwhile, was still quietly sitting there, contemplating me. I felt a deepening flush and wished I could excuse myself somehow to walk away and compose myself. 'So that's about it really-

'Except your surname.' He cut in.

I raised my eyebrows, surprised he had picked up on that missing info.

'Crossways.' I admitted, half smiling.

'Crossways? Really? Good name … feels a little appropriate for us both right now, doesn't it? That we're both facing a crossway. Or a crossroad maybe, in our life.'

I stared at him, taken aback by his acute perception of me from just a few bland sentences I'd thrown out. The need to move away became greater. I needed distance, if just for a moment.

'I'm hungry, fancy some chips?' Without waiting for a reply, I scurried off, inwardly cursing myself. Why couldn't I be braver? Why do I always do that when people want to get close to me? I despair of myself, I really do.

As the evening wore on we finally tackled head on the unmentioned subject. I raised their mum as a possible source in finding Natalie.

'Would she know or could think of anything to help us, even if it might seem insignificant or irrelevant?'

David looked reluctant. 'I don't want to upset her, you know? We don't … mention her much.'

His eyes told me more than any words could; that by not mentioning her had caused untold sorrow on them both. Yet right now all I had to go on was a very strong and very persistent gut feeling - and it was urging me to keep pushing this forward.

'I understand … but still I think we should talk to her. Or you could on your own if that would be easier.' I persisted. 'I just feel your mum may hold the key, perhaps without even knowing it.'

He was frowning hard at me, his lips pressed tight together. I began to regret my relentless persistence on this, so unlike me.

David half nodded. 'Maybe.' he replied in a non committal way.

I knew when to quit. To distract us, I reached down into the chip basket. Only one now lay sorrowfully there. I picked it up, broke it into two, then with a smile offered half to him. He looked touched and surprised by this. Then with a trace of a smile, he slowly reached out to take it.

The next morning I woke up early, before dawn, my mind restless with all that had happened in the last twenty four hours.

She was real, she was *real*. Wow, I still couldn't really believe it. She wasn't some crazy notion I had conjured up, but had lived and breathed and connected with people right here in Dingle. And her name was Natalie. Natalie, who had a family who loved her, who missed her. Surely there wasn't no greater confirmation for me then this; that I had made the right choice in following her!

With these staggering thoughts, David slipped easily in - no surprise there. Everything felt like it was revolving around him, as well as Natalie. And I wasn't sure how I felt about that.

I wonder if he has woken up with the same thoughts? Thoughts about me? If he too is lying in bed replaying yesterday's events, trying to make sense of this crazy exhausting roller-coaster of emotions we had lived through? I somehow sensed that he was, that even now as he washed and dressed, he was trying to work it through, all the while aware he would need to contact his mum today.

We had arranged to meet up after the lunchtime rush had ended. I knew no expectations had been placed on me to do anything to move this forward in the meantime. But I couldn't rest, or sit still, was finding it impossible to concentrate on a novel. After a few minutes of rereading the same paragraph I threw the book down in despair 'This is ridiculous!' I breathed out. It was only 9.53am for crying out loud!

The walls were beginning to close in around me. And I couldn't stand it a moment longer. I reached down to grab my bag and hotfooted it downstairs, spotting Ciara as I did.

'Hello there, my lovely!' She called out cheerfully as she cleared away the last of the breakfast plates. She stopped and gave me an approving glance. 'And in fact you are looking lovely as it happens.'

I glanced down at my red summer dress that had barely seen the light of day since impulsively purchasing it a couple of years ago. 'Oh thanks. You don't often see me in a dress.' I felt the need to explain.

'Well the dress is nice, that's true. But I was talking more about the glow in your cheeks.' She grinned, cocking her head, 'Someone put it there maybe?'

Feeling a tell tale blush creeping over me, I hastily smiled and backed out of the house. Her deep laughter followed me down the path.

As I disappeared down the hill, I never heard the abrupt dying away of Ciara's laughter as she gazed after me, or the sudden acute longing in her own eyes.

The day was just beautiful. I took a moment to breathe it in, allowing it to strengthen me.

Finding a quiet bench beside the quay harbour, I sat down, pulled out my laptop and began the task of google searching for the missing persons website.

Clicking on the link, I frowned hard as I saw countless faces of people flicker up, whose loved ones was desperate to find them just like we were. Unexpected tears grabbed the back of my throat. I swallowed them down, forced myself to focus on what was important here.

I found the right place to enter in Natalie's name and moments later a smiling, slightly grainy, out of date colour picture appeared. David had mentioned they had put her on as many sites as they could when she first went missing. I wanted to see if anyone had made any enquiries, or commented on this main one. But nothing. No sightings.

A telephone number was listed at the top of the website. I pressed the number into my mobile and after a few tooth pulling minutes of trying to get through to a live voice I finally got through to a lady called Emma, who was very friendly and patient but not able to help much as no-one had been in contact about Natalie. I thanked her, hung up. A heavy feeling weighed down on me as I dully watched the sun being eclipsed by a stray cloud. *How can we possibly find a woman who has hidden herself so successfully away for five years?* Or, even worse to comprehend - and I almost didn't want to allow this thought to enter the conscious air - *what if there was a more sinister reason for her disappearance?*

I felt myself gasp, aghast at even thinking this, a sick feeling filling the pit of my stomach. *No, surely not, I wont believe that!* She appeared to me, and she had felt *real, alive.* Of that I would stake my own life upon. I may not have a deep faith or understanding, but I knew that.

It was if the sky itself was confirming my resolution for the sun burst out then, its rays spreading a welcoming warmth over me. I closed my eyes to enjoy the delicious feeling of it stroking my skin.

A Catholic church, across from where I sat, suddenly caught my attention. Or, more precisely, the woman opening its wooden chapel doors did. She seemed stooped over, as if weighed down by a burden, as she struggled to push open its heavy doors. I half rose as if to go and help her, but as I did she managed to heave it open. There was a loud noise as it clanged shut behind her.

Curious, I walked across to the church. It was beautifully ornate, well cared for. I felt a strange stirring to go in. But I didn't want to disturb the woman, so though my hand hovered over the door handle, I let it fall away. *Another time..*

I spent the rest of the morning researching the internet, reading one real life story after another of how lost relatives had been found, and it gave me hope. There seemed no rhyme or reason to it; some coming back of their own accord, others taking on a new identity, some relatives hiring private detectives to do the complex solving. *Mmm I wonder if David or his mum ever used one?* I made a mental note to ask him later.

My phone beeped as I made my way to Cafe Peak. I peered at the screen and saw I had a missed call from my mum, as well as a text asking if I was okay and would I call.

Biting my lip, I felt that same peculiar sense of guilt towards my mum, as if I had upset her in some way without intending to. Yet why was that? She was an independent lady, and had instilled in me the same attribute. If anything I would have imagined her applauding this bold move of mine to come here.

And yet...

Sighing, I dialled her number. It was picked up on the second ring. 'Sweetheart? Is that you?'

'Of course its me, mum!' I said, shaking my head, a little perplexed by this anxiousness. 'Are you okay? Its not like you to be trying to contact me so urgently.'

Instead of answering me, she said, 'I could ask you the same. Its not like you to drop everything like this. What are you doing there in Dingle?!'

'I know, I know, sounds off the wall. But don't worry, okay? I'm helping David find his sister-'

'David? *David who?* '

'Carson .. but I don't think you would know him. We're looking for his sister, Natalie.'

There was a silence on the other end. A strange disconcerting silence. Frowning, I waited for a moment. Still nothing. I felt a mild alarm sweep through me.

'Mum, are you still there?! What's happened?'

Her voice was faint, as if calling from a long distance. 'Yes, yes I'm still here.'

Greg walked past and called out a hello to me. I distractedly waved back while forcing a note of cheerfulness into my voice. 'Oh good, had me worried there for a moment! Listen, really don't worry about me, I'm fine. I'll call you later. …' I paused then felt compelled to add 'Love you.' Then when the silence dragged on, 'Ok, bye then.'

I strained to hear a 'Bye' before reluctantly disconnecting the call. 'Odd.' I muttered, staring at the phone as if it could offer me an explanation.

'So you didn't bugger off on the first ferry out of here then...'

I looked up. David stood in the doorway of his cafe, hands on hips where his black apron was tied. His face was unreadable in the shadows, but I sensed behind the flippant humour lay a touch of vulnerability.

'It was fully booked.' I quipped, 'Plus of course, it would be a waste of my airline ticket.'

A smile touched the corners of his mouth. I couldn't help responding in kind.

'Ah well, guess you'll just have to cope with our Irish hospitality a little longer then, wont you? Till the next plane comes in, of course...'

'It's true I do have the airline on speed dial, just in case.'

Pushing aside niggling concerns about mum, I slowly walked up to a softly laughing David.

Chapter Eight

I could feel his anxiety washing over us like a high tide as we walked towards her house, and felt compelled to ask him, yet again. 'Are you sure you wouldn't find this easier on your own?'

David shook his head vehemently. 'Definitely not. I need you here.' He turned to look at me. 'You're my legitimate reason for bringing Nat up.'

'Or more like the fall girl if it all goes belly up.' came my wry response, feeling my insides knot into a tangled mess. Perhaps "lamb to the slaughter" would be more appropriate...

'Mm... I'd prefer to call you my safety net.'

'Not any more reassuring, David. Safety nets have a tendency to snag and break.'

'Ah, don't you be worrying, she's a pussy cat, my mam.'

'A pussy cat who will be after me to be fish bait!'

David burst out laughing, unable to help himself. The heartwarming sound dispelled our anxiousness for one brief glorious moment.

We arrived outside a small, quite ordinary looking white terrace house, tucked neatly between similar looking homes. A sombre feel swept over us, as we stood staring at the door to, I guess, try to put off the inevitable. After a small pregnant pause, David finally took the lead and jogged up to the front door, me trailing behind, letting himself in with his own front key while he shouted out 'Only me, mam.'

I heard a surprised exclamation, followed by a petite lady emerging from what appeared to be the sitting room to greet us in the hallway. The hallway itself lacked natural light, so giving the impression of being smaller in size then it actually was. Her dark hair was sprinkled with grey and just skimmed her shoulders. It was immediately clear David had inherited her eyes, though hers a touch more darkened.

'Davey my lovely! I wasn't expecting you!' She was kissing his cheek, clearly delighted to see him. As David gave her a quick hug, her eyes collided with mine. She stepped back in surprise, a little flustered, narrowly missing tripping over the bottom carpeted stairs that led up to the first floor. As our eyes met, a strange, odd feeling- or maybe a sensation - came over me. Something about her seemed very familiar, exactly the same feeling, in fact, as when I first met David. Perhaps she reminded me of someone I'd met before, maybe? Or her daughter-

Her voice broke into my incoherent haphazard thoughts.

'Oh… I'm sorry, I didn't know Dave had someone with him. '

David turned to introduce me. 'This is Lily, a … friend. A new friend. Kind of.' He shot me an apologetic look, the tiniest shrug to his shoulders as if to say *how else can I introduce you?*

My well instilled manners, drummed into me from a young age, rose up to save us from any further awkwardness. I smiled, extended out my hand. 'Hi, it's nice to meet you, Mrs Carson.'

'Oh now, call me Iona.'

David showed me into the lounge before ushering his very intrigued mum into the kitchen 'to put the kettle on'. I gazed around me, taking in my surroundings. The room was by no means elaborate or full of knick knacks. It was simply furnished with practical, hardy chairs, as well as a small sofa and a table, with papers scattered across it, pushed into one corner. I could only see the fewest of personal touches, mostly a few photos of David and Natalie. Strangely, there was none of his Dad, or them as a married couple. At least, not in this room.

I was drawn towards a photo of David, proudly displayed centre stage on the fireplace, and stepped closer to peer at it. There he stood on the doorway to 'Cafe Peak', a proud grin across his face, his arms flung out in jubilation. In the background, colourful balloons and 'Grand Opening' banners filled the air around him, with excited faces bouncing around him, some with raised coffee cups as if saluting. I smiled. His pride and joy was evident, contagious.

My finger traced along the fireplace and hovered when it came to a photo of Natalie. *That's why no-one recognised her from my photo!* I gasped, taking in her short blond spiky hair, her black heavy eye lined eyes and thin face, *so different from how she looks now with those long dark locks the same as her brother*. It was a candid shot, taken almost unawares by the subject. Her head was slightly turned away and there was a wide smile on her face directed towards someone outside of the shot. I felt my breath catch; the contrast from this to the haunted desperate look she had shown me in the photo was staggering. *Who had brought such a stunning smile to her face here? Such tenderness to her eyes?*

My thoughts were interrupted by the clear sound of their voices carrying over to me, the whistling kettle having been switched off and with it their cover.

'So she's not your new girl?'

'No, mam, no, nothing like that! You know after Abby I'm not looking. Lily's here to .. help us with something.'

'Oh! ... Should I be worried?'

There was a pause, then 'Let's go through, hey?'

I forced myself to unfreeze my body from the fireplace as I heard their footsteps approach. I tried to appear nonchalant and relaxed as they came in. I must have failed badly though, because when my eyes connected with David's he gave me an arched look. I forced a smile out before perching, uncomfortably, on the first seat I could reach.

As we sipped our tea, Iona looked from David to me expectantly. I looked expectantly at David, he to me, each clearly waiting for the other to start. My look turned vehement. David threw it back at me, ten fold. The silence became unbearably loud. I heard a sigh and, startled, turned towards it.

Iona shook her head softly. 'Well now, I was never one for silence, as my lad here will tell you. So why don't you just spit it out, Lily.' came the command

More than a little thrown the attention was all directed towards me (earning a visibly relieved David a hot daggering look he

51

studiously ignored) I began, in a halting voice, to explain the reason in why she found me here, sitting here in her lounge, about to unleash new emotional distress on her.

Have you ever watched someone literally shrink away in front of your very eyes? Just withdraw into a place deep within them where no pain or hurt can get to them ... a place they know so intimately they can locate it in a breath?

I watched this happening to Iona as I stammered on. There was the quietest intake of breath, a startled look leading to an unbridled hope... before it was painfully extinguished. I saw anguish. And then I saw her emotions completely shut down, a defence mechanism that's impossible to force open again.

I'm not sure what reaction I expected. Or hoped for. A part of me had dared to believe she would welcome me with open arms on this positive "sighting". At least with David, it had been brutal, but real, and had given me a fighting chance. With Iona there was ... nothing.

Just nothing. The silence grew loud and unbearable. Despairing, I turned to David who was staring hard at his mum. *Come on, say something!*.

Finally, he tentatively reached out to take her hand. She flinched at the touch but didn't pull away.

'Mam... mam look at me.'

Slowly she turned to him.

He recoiled back a little.

'Say something, anything. But don't shut me out right now, mam!' He urged, pleaded, 'We're not bringing this up to cause you pain for the sake, but because we think, we believe that Nat wants us to find her.'

Iona stared hard at her earnest son. His eyes were bright with unshed tears, but there was no emotion in hers. I found that oddly strange... and a little chilling.

'What do you want me to say?' came her slow empty reply. 'That I believe you, that we should rush out now to find her, is that it?' She suddenly gripped his hand in a painful crush. 'Listen to me, son...

she does not want to be found.' Each word was punctuated out. I saw David flinch at the brutal way it was delivered.

'Don't say that.' He whispered, 'Mam, please try to understand what we are telling you-'

'I don't want to hear anymore, David. And I don't want us to fall out over this. I think it would be best if you and your friend leave now. We'll talk later.'

Iona was already standing up, letting go of her son's hand.

My eyes were beseeching as I stared at David. Nothing about this felt right. There was more in her eyes. Her reaction too controlled. *Almost as if she hadn't been surprised at all...*

David looked lost as he gave me a half despairing shrug. 'I don't want to leave you upset.'

Iona shook her head. 'I'm not upset, my bairn. I just don't think we should talk about this again.' She turned to me. I braced myself. Yet she gave me a polite smile, holding out her hand. 'Now I'm sorry we couldn't have met in better circumstances, Lily - sorry, I don't think I caught your last name.'

'Crossways, its Lily Crossways.' I mumbled, taking the proffered hand.

I felt the jolt of shock startle us both. She took a small step back. Her eyes widened as she took me in. At last I had a real emotive reaction from her... but from my name? *I don't understand. Mum reacted the same way to me when I said David's surname!*

'Did you ... have you ... visited Dingle before?' Came the quiet reply, her eyes burning my face.

'When I was a child, we came here on holiday a couple of times, I think.' I kept her eyes locked with mine, willing them to reveal more to me.

David had been half listening to our conversation but his mind was still on Nat. 'Okay, I'll call you tomorrow, mam, if that's what you'd prefer.'

At the sound of his voice, the fragile cord was broken. She released my hand, her eyes turning away. David gently steered me towards the door, and took my hand. The unexpected touch of him against my skin sent a tingle up my arm.

At the open doorway, David turned back. He waited until his mum's eyes met his, then said with a firmness I couldn't help admiring, "We're not giving up on this, mam. She wants to be found, I know it, *I feel it*. We're not mad! I saw her appear with my own eyes on Lily's photo, for crying out loud, when I definitely know she wasn't there when we took it! I can't shrug this off or pretend it didn't happen. It has happened. Maybe someone up there is trying to send us a message, and I can't live with myself if I don't do everything in my power to try and find her. What if she is in trouble, mam?' At those last words his voice broke a little. I saw Iona was physically moved, though she tried hard to cover it.

She gave a slight nod, said nothing. My heart went out to David. He had wanted so much more. He gave a little sigh then reached down and kissed Iona's pale cheek. We turned to leave.

The front door clicked shut behind us. We walked off a little way. I looked up at David, and squeezed his hand where it still held mine. I wanted to give him comfort, but struggled with the right words to say.

He seemed to understand this and turned to give a faint smile. I smiled back, touching my cheek against his arm for the briefest moment.

'I'm sorry I landed you in it back there, leaving it all to you, you know? I just… didn't know how to begin.'

'Mmm… don't think you're completely off the hook there. That was particularly despicable. But I do understand, sort of.' I gave him a little grin, then added, more seriously. 'We *will* find your sister. Another path will open up, you'll see.'

David swallowed, nodded, stared straight ahead. 'We have to, Lily, because we can't go back now. God knows we can't hide from the truth. It's too late for that.'

It was busy in the "Smugglers" when we walked in. Tourists and locals mingled in happy company. David moved us confidently through the hoards, then turned at the sound of his name being shouted over the din.

'Dave, over here mate!' A brown haired man, sitting with a petite blond lady, was enthusiastically beckoning us over, grinning.

On seeing who it was, David waved back, then bent close to my ear. 'Up for meeting my crazy mate?!'

'I'm beginning to suspect you are all nutters round here. But yes, lead the way...'

Immediately the two men threw themselves into that strange 'side on side hug while slapping each other on the back' ritual that seems to be adopted by men across the world. Only then did he remember shy little me, standing there like some gooseberry.

'Guys meet Lily! Lily, this is my very good friend Sean and his gorgeous wife Amy.'

Amy blushed prettily at this, turning to smile quietly at me. 'Hello.'

I smiled at them both. 'Nice to meet you.'

'And you, Lily.' Sean commented amusingly while his unsubtle eyebrows made wild obscene gestures at David. David punched Sean on the arm, while muttering, 'Shut up!'

Sean magically produced two chairs from nowhere, and I slipped my coat over one, finding this all a little bemusing.

'What will you be having then, Lily?' Sean was asking me without really looking directly at me, as he moved to go to the bar. This tiny bit of rudeness annoyed me for reasons I couldn't put a name to.

Give him a chance, I scolded myself and to make amends, with a funny need to make a good impression myself, I put out a hand to stop him.

'No, no! Let me. What would you all like?'

'Well, in that case, it would be rude to refuse you.' Sean shrugged, already sitting down. 'Greg will know our usuals.'

'You need any help getting yourself to the bar?' David felt compelled to check, though already settling himself nicely into the chair, stretching lazily back.

I raised an eyebrow. 'I'm sure I can manage. If not, Greg will come to my rescue, I'm sure.'

I left the three of them, the boys' raucous laughter following me, their closeness evident. I felt an acute envy, which I pushed quickly down.

Through sheer determination, I squeezed my way through sharp elbows to reach the sanctuary of the bar. I spotted Greg amongst the bartenders conjuring up drinks in spellbinding seconds, and waited patiently amongst strangers like myself until he finally spotted me. When he did, his face lit up, cheering me up no end.

'Are you not allowed a day off?!' I teased, grinning as I leaned on the bar.

'Well now, seeing as I actually own the place, I kind of feel obliged to be here most of the time.'

'Oh!' I exclaimed, shocked, 'I had no idea you actually owned it!'

'I know, I look too young and crease free to have this responsibility. But to finish answering your question, I do give myself time off, as I believe you bore witness to yesterday. Want to have a tour around with me when I next have a free one?'

'Oh!' I found myself repeating, taken aback. It hadn't sounded like a date, offered so casually like that, but there was a spark of anticipation in his eyes which sort of hinted at his real intention. My natural reaction was to withdraw. Fast. *Yet...* 'Okay, that would be nice .' I instead found myself replying, realising I meant every word. It would be nice to have an easy going, no expectation friendship with this man. *As long as it was just that.*

Greg looked pleased, then asked, 'Dave want his usual?'

'Yes, please. And his friends Sean and Amy. They said you would know what they drink?'

'I do indeed. And I know yours too, English girl.'

It was a few minutes before I finally made it back to the table, clinging on tightly to the tray so as not to spill one drop of the "nectar of the gods", as it was referred to here.

They looked up and David smiled as, sweating a little, I gingerly put the tray down with relief.

'Ah! You can come join us any time bringing us gifts like this. And look!' Sean commented, grabbing his pint, 'She evens brings us crisps.'

'Actually, Greg gave them to us as a little freebie.' I felt compelled to correct as I passed David's drink to him, who accepted with a 'Thanks', then gave Amy her drink, who quietly mumbled, 'Thank you.'

'Us ...or to you?' Sean joked, giving David a cheeky sideways glance. David gave a tight unamused smile back. I just decided to ignore his comment and concentrate on taking my coat off.

'You've obviously made a good impression.' David mumbled so only I could hear as I slid into the seat next to him, left empty. His blue eyes briefly made contact with mine. 'I only give free cake to customers I really, *really* like.'

My breath quickened. 'Would I qualify for free cake yet?' I softly replied, surprising myself with the note of flirtation behind it.

A current passed between us. It seemed a long time before he finally answered. 'You would.'

Two simple words. But said with such meaning. I felt a rush go through my body.

The not so subtle coughing coming in the direction of Sean unfortunately had its desired effect.

'Nice of you to join us again. So how come Amy and I don't get free cake then?!'

'Now that, as you know, is a downright lie, my friend! You're both eating my profits away.' David protested, and the mood was light again.

Conversation flowed easily, and within time, Amy came out of her natural reticence and started to engage with me. I think she was glad to have some female conversation, especially as the men's talk was becoming more crass as the 'nectar' flowed.

Her voice had a soft Irish tilt that reminded me of warm hazy sun. I found myself bending closer to catch her words.

'How are you finding it here in Dingle? I hope we're making you feel welcome.'

I smiled warmly. 'You have.' My eyes glanced towards David as I spoke. 'At least, more so now as we go along. '

Amy gave me a quizzable look, no doubt trying to understand my underlying message. But to begin to try and explain my presence here caused a sudden sharp headache to erupt across my forehead.

After a polite pause, Amy smiled back. 'Well, I'm glad you're settling in.' Small hesitation then, 'I don't remember Dave mentioning having known you before...''

'Well, no... we're only really just getting to know each other. I did holiday here a few weeks back, but just for a few days. Oh, and when I was a child we came here as a family.' I found myself adding, perhaps unnecessarily, but Amy had this way of getting you to keep talking, merely by the fact she said nothing. It was a trick I often used myself, to ensure the spotlight remained off me. Now I was being played by my own game... and I wasn't sure it was a great feeling. I heard myself rambling on. 'It's so beautiful here, I really love it. Have you and Sean always lived here?' I finally got in, determined to shift the spotlight onto her.

She gave a small smile. 'For a long time, yes.' Amy's eyes swung to her husband who was animatedly describing something to a laughing David. A small frown creased her otherwise smooth pale skin. 'Sean likes it here. He wants us to stay here.'

Something in her tone stopped me short from making a comment. I watched a pulse flicker on her neck, before she turned almost reluctantly back to me.

For the briefest of moments I saw something in her eyes that made me inwardly catch my breath ... like a deer trapped in headlights. Then it was gone and I wondered if it was merely my overactive imagination. Or too much drink.

I mentally shrugged it off and the conversation turned to easier subjects. I was just telling Amy about living in Brighton when we became aware David and Sean had abruptly stopped talking. Surprised, we both turned to look at them.

Sean was staring at David. His body had grown taut, immobile, his features unreadable. All trace of his carefree voice had gone. 'You're doing what? '

David pushed aside his forgotten beer and quietly repeated himself. 'Lily and I have started looking for her.' He reached out towards his friend, 'I know its a shock and all, but its what I need to do. So try and be that supportive mate you always are.'

Sean was slowly shaking his head, completely stunned. 'I can't believe you're doing this.' I heard him half whisper. He suddenly grabbed a startled David by the arm. His voice was staggeringly fierce, harsh even. 'Don't do this, trust me on this mate. Don't do it. You're going to regret it-'

'No, it'll be fine.' David was hastening to reassure. I felt a lump in my throat as I watched them. David, then Sean, turned to look at me and I nodded, holding him in my gaze. There was a brief silence, then, 'Could somebody *please* tell me what you're all talking about!'

Broken out of our reverie, we all swung round to look at a tense, flushed faced Amy. Sean hesitated for the longest time, and I was beginning to wonder if I would have to tell her. Then, with a subdued voice he told her in what felt like a very cold voice.

In that moment, as we all stared at Amy, I finally understood the saying "as pale as a ghost". For that was exactly what she had looked like.

And later in bed, it was *her* face which prevailed my sleep, not Iona's as I would have thought. If you had asked me why, I couldn't have told you. But something wasn't *right*. I couldn't get away from the fact that their's had not been a natural reaction to a friend's search for his sister, even if they were genuinely concerned he was setting himself up for a disappointment. Even if they had all been very close as friends, and still upset at her missing.

Did they know more? Against all perceivable thought and beggaring belief were they somehow still in touch with her? And there was something about Sean I just didn't trust.

Surely though they couldn't have kept a big secret hidden from David all this time!?

Lily, stop! You're reading way too much into this. You know you're hopeless at reading people's reactions, emotions. Of course they're going to be shocked by news like this. .. anyone would be.

Let it go. Just let it go. At least for now. No good is going to come from thinking this way. You need to concentrate on what you know and what's important. That's all you need to do for now.

Chapter Nine

I was feeling buoyed up, determined to find Natalie now, no matter what. I couldn't let David down – I mean Natalie, of course I mean Natalie.

David and I spent the next couple of evenings, fuelled by Ciara's irish coffees, trying to piece together what David remembered from just before she'd left them. He thought there had been some boyfriend that Nat had been seeing, but frustratingly could remember very little about what she had told David about this mystery man.

'But do you think he could have had something to do with ... well her disappearing?' I dared to broach.

A look of alarm darkened his eyes. 'What do you mean, something to do with it?'

I grimaced, suddenly unsure where I was going with this. 'Just thinking aloud, okay? Secretive relationship, then disappearing without a word ...'

'And there's nothing in hell we can do to find out if that was the case.'

'Maybe your mum might remember him?' I asked, hopeful.

David looked less so, shooting me a pained face. 'Don't bank on it, Lil. Mam and Nat didn't really have the most ... harmonious of relationships, if you get what I mean. Think more slanging matches and doors banging then cosy chats by the fire.'

I gave a short laugh.'Okay, I see your point, but it would still be worth mentioning next time you see her. '

An answering short grunt as good as it was going to get in acknowledgement to this, I tried a different angle.

'What about close friends who still live round here who might know something?'

David stared at me. There was a sudden hard note in his eyes. 'If there was a "friend"' this word was empathised in such a way it left me in no doubt of his meaning, 'who knew all this time where my sister was, knowing the heartache it had caused my mam, let's just say you wouldn't want to be that person when I caught up with them.'

He looked away, his jaw clenching. I stared at him for a moment. 'I wouldn't blame you.' I said quietly. He swung back to me, surprised, before giving me a faint smile. 'Any other brainwaves in that busy head of yours?'

I wish I did...

'I'm working on it.' I said instead, letting out a long breath. A sudden thought flew into my foggy head. 'Are you on Facebook?'

David gave a derisive snort. 'You're not anyone if you're not on facebook these days don't you know. Not that I've exactly got any blimin' time to snoop in on other people's lives, some of us actually have a business-'

I cut in before he went into a full blown rant about social media and all. 'Well, now I need you to. I think you should private message all your friends – I'm presuming you do actually have friends on your facebook page?'

'Oh ha ha.' Came the sarcastic reply.

I bit back a smile. 'Good. Just get the feelers out. I know its a long shot ...'

'Yeah, yeah, I'm with you.'

Oh my goodness, was that finally an agreement to one of my suggestions? I nearly fell off my armchair in shock. All other thoughts flitted away with this rather momentous step forward. Best not to push it any further tonight.

Not long after, when it was closing on nine pm, David made his excuses and left.

I was just making my way slowly upstairs, feeling a twinge of a headache developing behind my eyes, when I bumped into Ciara, looking a little more glamourous then normal.

'Wow, look at you!' I exclaimed in admiration, 'Are you off somewhere nice ... with someone nice maybe?' I fished.

Then immediately regretted my nosiness as I watched a moment of pain darken her eyes, before they returned back to their normal light. *Had I seen that right?* Or was it a trick of the evening sun streaming in through the downstairs hallway?

'With a girlfriend, yes! We thought we deserved a little drink out, you know.'

'Most definitely you do!' I agreed, smiling.

'Now don't be waiting up for me, my lovely!'

'No, don't worry I wont! Say hi to Greg for me if you pop into the "Smugglers".' I added as I made my way up the stairs.

It was only afterwards, as I closed my bedroom door and flung myself onto the soft welcoming contours of my bed, that it occurred to me Ciara never answered my last comment.

It's the same woman, I'm sure of it!

Without thinking, I bolted up from the bench I had now adopted as my own, and darted across the road to the church doors, just catching it and almost tearing off what was left of my nails, before it slammed shut.

Inside, the air was still, the light a little dimmer. I took a moment to adjust my eyes to its subdued hush.

She must be here, I saw her come in!

Not five minutes ago, I had been sitting polishing off a slightly stale cheese sandwich as I idled away lunchtime the next day, frustrated by my lack of progress in ringing round the local police stations to see if they knew Natalie Carson, when something unexplained had caused me to look sharply up. And there she was, the slightly stooped over woman wearing a head scarf making her way into her church, only this time looking more familiar to my senses.

There! There she is.

Before courage failed me, I walked up behind her, as she stood staring up at the glass painted window of Mary and Jesus. We were alone in the little church.

I hesitated as to whether I should tap her on the shoulder, but instead opting for a not so discreet clearing of my throat.

63

I held my breath as she turned around. Then we both gave a little gasp.

There was a long silence, then Iona frowned a little as she stared at me. 'Lily? Is Davey with you? Are you-'

'No, no, just me.' I broke in .

She still stared at me. 'I didn't know you prayed.'

'I don't, well not really ... ' I felt compelled to admit. 'But I wish I did more, if that makes sense.'

Iona nodded a little, swallowed, looked away. 'Yes, yes it does.'

She's troubled. Her heart is so heavy. Is there more? There has to be more going on here.

I cleared my throat again, trying hard to find the right words. Everything in me screamed to turn around and run away. I loathed confrontation of any kind.

But then, right there in front of my eyes, I saw Natalie's vivid face, clearly, starkly, her desperation piercing my heart as she had stared at me. Without thinking, I blurted out, 'Are you sure you don't know where Natalie might be?'

She spun round. I stepped back against the full throttle force of her overwhelming anger. 'Of course I don't! Why are you asking me that?! Do you not think that every fibre of me wants to see my daughter again, know she's okay?!'

'I'm sorry, so sorry, I didn't mean to upset you.' I hastily retreated, taking a step back.

'Please, let me be so that I can pray in peace.'

Nodding, I turned and walked quickly to the heavy door, forcing it open. Yet, just as I went to step out its the brightness, something propelled me to stop, to turn.

Iona stood there staring at me, her body rigid to the spot. It seemed a great effort to turn her head away, bending it down low.

As if in shame..

Chapter Ten

It was already nearing the end of my first week here in Dingle. And the stark simple truth was this - we were no nearer to finding Natalie then we were a few days ago. That was the inescapable fact, the truth I had to face up to.

And my goodness, I don't know what to do, how to make this happen, how to make this *right*. I can feel, right now, a hard inner battle being fought in my mind and was becoming more painfully obvious the insistent rational side of me was wearing down the newly discovered battle-weary optimistic side; one crushing step at a time. So many thoughts were cramming their way into my bruised head. It wasn't just the constant niggling worry of money, which seemed to be draining out of my purse at an alarming rate. Nor was it that ever concerning thought that there may not be a job waiting for me back home. Or even the lure of my safe, comfortable life I'd left behind.

No, no what scared me the most was what I was losing – my resolve to find Natalie, in a world that frankly cared little. And I hated it. So much. Hated that I could be so weak, cave in this fast. The thought of walking away from David, of giving up... well, it literally made me feel sick. He was relying heavily on me, had opened up to me despite the painfulness of it, was even now looking to me to keep his own determination and resolve alive. He had far more right then me to give up.

What can I do? What can *I do!* I'm seriously out of my depth here. My gut feeling had me convinced that his mum was the clue to unlocking this. But I'd obviously been wrong in that theory. Then I was convinced I'd read more into Sean and Amy's reaction to our news, but David assures me they know no more then we do. Every avenue we've tried since has us coming up against an impossible brick wall, either through bureaucracy, red tape or simply nobody knowing anything. David had had lots of sympathy messages on

65

Facebook, but nothing firm to go on, just a couple of possible 'sightings' in Cork.

I'm going to let you down, David. And I can't bear that, because I care too much for you now, and that's not something which I can stop. Believe me I tried to. It feels like you're consuming my every thought. And that scares me. I'm not a fool, I know your feelings couldn't be more different to mine. I'm just a girl whose helping you find your sister and who will one day soon go back to her normal life. But still, I don't want you to forever remember me as the girl who crushingly let you down.

God, I'm begging you, you need to step in and do something, *anything* to stop this stagnate*!*

My feet and body felt weary as I slowly walked down to the breakfast room. My eyes felt raw, as did my throat, from the ache, I think, of frustrated unshed tears.

Ciara was as cheerful as ever as she greeted me, pouring tea into a guest's cup. I gave a wan smile in return as I sat at my favourite table by the front bay window, which overlooked the distant mountains. The sight of them humbled me.

'Well now my lovely, you look like you need a strong cup of your English tea. Not slept so well?'

Ciara was there, looking down at me, as I turned my head. Though she smiled, I could see the concern in her grey eyes; and that was nearly the undoing of me. I couldn't talk for fear the tears would break free of the fragile restraint I had on them, so instead just shook my head.

Ciara bent down, stroked my shoulder for a moment, then poured my tea into her pretty wedgewood cup. 'I'll bring you some warm toast and jam. Just what you need.'

I nodded gratefully, blinking, then turned back to the window, trying to get a grip on my emotions. I never cried, ever. Not even when Dad died. I actually thought that part of my emotions had permanently shut down in me. *What was happening to me?* All at once, as I stared down at my hands, I felt like I was looking down on myself, if that made sense, staring in sheer disbelief at this unmet

66

fragile woman who wanted to be strong, yet all too aware of her own weakness and limitations. I tried to shake myself out of it, grabbing my cup with a slight shaky hand.

I was halfway through one piece of toast, eaten more out of politeness then genuine hunger, when my phone began to buzz. I reached down and pulled it out of my jeans, half deciding to cut off whoever it was. I looked at the screen, all ready to hit the decline button.

It was David.

I hesitated for the briefest second, then pressed accept. I cleared my throat before saying

'Hi, how- '

'Lily? Are you free right now?'

His voice was hurried, urgent. Frowning, I pressed the phone closer to my ear. 'I can be.'

'Good, good. Come to the cafe as soon as.'

'Okay, but what's so urgent?' My heart leaped. 'Do you have a lead?'

'Maybe.' A short bated pause that had me holding my breath, then 'Mam called me. She says she has something that might help...'

My heart zinged, danced. The tears came joyfully to my eyes. I knew in that moment my prayer had just been answered.

'Don't expect too much from her.' I quietly said as Iona answered the door to us barely twenty minutes later.

David kissed his mum on the cheek. We shared a quick look as we followed Iona into the lounge.

Iona looked at her son for a long time. She seemed to be preparing herself, mentally composing in her head what she was about to say. It seemed to be causing her pain. I watched a tide of emotions flow over her, before she finally spoke. My body tensed.

'Davey, my love, there's something I've not shared with you and it was wrong of me. I know that now - no, don't say anything yet, let me finish.' Iona took a deep breath, sat down, with us following suit.

I kept looking from mother to son. David was holding his breath, his eyes never straying from his mum's face.

'About two years ago I heard from your sister. In a letter.' She rushed on, reaching out a hand to her son, whose sharp intake of breath from this confession had both of us looking at him in concern. 'She said she was fine, not to worry, told me she was living in Cork -'

David half rose from the chair. 'Did it have an address? Why didn't you go straight to her?! Or call me, I would have gone-'

Iona pushed him gently back down. 'Because she said she was moving that week and by the time I got this letter she would have moved on. Believe me son, I wanted to! But what good would that have done, huh? She didn't want to come home, for whatever reason, but at least I knew she was alive. Oh, the relief of that! Do you understand, love?'

Her eyes were pleading with him, and my heart moved a little for her. She obviously knew she had made the wrong choice on so many levels. But would I have acted in the same way?

David was shaking his head, trying hard to fight down a need to shout at his mum. The hurt in his eyes must be cutting deep into Iona's own heart right then. He swore under his breath.

'I can't believe this.' He half whispered, 'All this time you knew she was alive and you never said a word even when I poured out my fears to you-'

Iona swallowed hard, still clinging onto his reluctant hand. 'I know, son. I'm so sorry... I...' Her voice trailed weakly off.

I cleared my throat, breaking in gently, though part of me wanted to shout at this woman for her misguided loyalty. Two years was a long time, damn it! Anything could have happened since.

'Why are you telling David now, Iona? What's changed?'

Her head swung up, almost startled to realise I was sitting there. 'I, ah, I haven't slept since you came over last week asking for my help. Telling me my daughter was calling out for me. I see her in my dreams… crying.' Her voice broke. She turned her head away. 'Then when you followed me to the church, Lily, and I saw in your eyes you knew, you knew...'

David stared at her, before closing his eyes for a moment. When he opened them again I felt he had won some internal battle over himself. His voice was calmer, more measured. I admired him more than I ever had, knew my heart was falling just one more step towards him.

'Mam, mam, look at me.' She slowly turned to him, her eyes raw and red. 'It's alright, its okay. You've done the right thing in telling me. Do you still have the letter?' When she nodded, he nodded too. 'Good, why don't you go get it for me?'

Iona slowly got up and walked out of the room. As she did, I moved closer to David, crouching down in front of him. His eyes turned to mine, and for a moment he lost his composure and in doing so, revealed the raw hurt his heart felt of this misguided loyalty, betrayal even, of his mother's. I took his hand and squeezed it, trying somehow to give him some of my own strength. His hand tightened around mine, then raised it to press it against his cheek. Our eyes held.

Iona walked back in, and he let go. I went to move away as Iona handed over the letter; her hand shaking as she did. But David stopped me, pulling me down next to him instead. He carefully took the letter out of the envelope, then held it up so we could both see it. It was short, barely covering one side of the paper. The writing was scrawled, heavy. There was a Cork address at the top.

Silently we read:

" *Hi mam*

Please don't worry about me. I'm okay. I'm sorry I've not been in touch. Trust me there's a reason for this which I can't tell you. It's the reason I had to leave so quickly. I'm living at this address at the moment but moving on in the new few days. I'll write to you again with my new address.

I love you and Dad and David and think of you all often.

Love your Nat xxx "

69

As I finished reading it, I turned to David. He was staring fiercely at the words as if they could tell him more, as if their very power alone could conjure Natalie up right there in this lounge. He quickly blinked, trying hard to compose himself.

'Okay, okay...' David let out a shuddering breath. 'Well, this is a start, right? We'll start with this address and see where the trail takes us.' He looked to me for confirmation. I nodded.

'But Davey my love, this was such a long time ago! It will lead to noth-'

'It will lead to something.' He cut in firmly. 'You'll have to trust me with this, mam.'

She stared at him then replied quietly, almost defensively, 'I do, I do trust you, son.'

At last we had something to go on! This energy sapping "nothingness" had been broken!

But it'd come at a cost. Something had been temporarily broken between mother and son. Oh, it was painful to see and I fervently hoped it would be just that; temporary. Though she'd been in the wrong, I felt I understood her reasons, wrong though they might have been. Yet it was easier for me, wasn't it, to be objective? I was an outsider to the family, being granted access in. How would I feel if it had been my mum keeping something so major, so profound as this from me?

David was still in a complete mind spin when we left. I took him back to my room at Ciara's, feeling this was better then going straight back to his café and having to be 'on show'. He half heartedly tried to rail against this idea.

'I need to get to the café, Dora is on her own.'

'She will be fine for another half an hour.' I firmly replied, almost bodily leading him to mine.

As we sat a little awkwardly on my bed, it being the only form of seating, I was reminded of the last time David had been here when he dared me to prove myself and the truth of my photos and action. His presence then had been daunting, overawing, almost threatening. Now it was tenderer then before, warmer ... and all too blatantly masculine. I could feel myself responding to his close proximity, a warm flush growing inside me. I felt a little flustered ... and aroused.

If he was physically aware of me in the same way, he was hiding it pretty damn well. *Good job I don't have a huge ego,* I mused, *David's not helping to boost it one bit.* An urge to suddenly kiss him, and see how he would react, was rather maddeningly trying to take over my senses. Jumping up in haste, I busied myself with the tea tray as the kettle finally, *finally* reached boiling point.

'Okay, drink this.' I said as I handed over the tea, proud of this simple accomplishment under the circumstances. 'Not quite up to your standards, of course.' I smiled.

'Ah, well, not everyone has my natural talent, its true.' He "humbly" joked, and I felt lighter for hearing this return to normality. 'Plus, only you strange English folk drink tea.' He added, half grimacing as he took a tiny polite sip.

'I argue against that, you poor naive Irish man! Tea was sent down from heaven, and more than superior to any coffee concoction you can produce! Drink all of that up and then dare to disagree with me.'

David raised one eyebrow, then accepting my challenge he took a long drawn out gulp of my tea. 'Its… actually, its not that bad.' He seemed perplexed by this discovery. 'At least you make it with a good strength to it.'

'Oh, can't be doing with milky tea.' I made a face, grimacing at the thought. 'So now you have discovered this truth you should employ me at your café to improve your tea connoisseur knowledge.' I half joked. 'I bet I could get your customers buying my tea over your coffee any day.'

His other eyebrow shot up. 'Is that so, is that so? Well maybe, Ms Crossways, I will challenge you to that... Though don't you need to be heading back soon?' He pressed on, looking intently at me.

I sat down heavily next to him, my euphoria crashing in an instant. 'Soon, yes.' I slowly answered, turning to look at him.

'But not yet?' He continued, a hurried note entering his voice.

'No, not yet. ' *Not yet...*

He continued to look at me for a long time. I found my breath catching, wondering what he would do next.

David put down his half finished cup, took my hand and brought it up to his mouth. His lips briefly touched my warm skin. 'I'm glad.' His voice was warm, sincere.

And then he was out of my room before I had any chance to respond, for my senses to catch up, calling out over his shoulder as he did. 'Get cracking on that address and report back to me at lunchtime, fiery.'

It hadn't been hard to locate the address on my googlemaps. We planned to go the following morning and I offered to drive us, feeling a strange need to be active rather than a restless passenger. Thinking I needed to feel refreshed tomorrow, I had every plan to have an early night. David was busy catching up on paperwork for his café, having fallen a little behind with recent events.

That was the plan, anyway. The reality was I found myself unable to sit still for longer then five minutes, let alone go to sleep, so bravely made the decision to go alone to Greg's pub. I'm not sure I've ever gone anywhere alone before, but it felt quite liberating, intoxicating even. Greg didn't disappoint. He kept me entertained from where I sat all evening on a very comfy black padded bar stall, as well as nicely fed and watered. After a second rather large glass of rose wine inside me, accompanied by a surprising kiss on my flushed cheek from Greg, I felt relaxed enough to drag myself back to Ciara's and to my welcoming bed, eager to sleep.

But sleep, when it came, was fragmented, full of vivid images colliding with each other. I kept looking for Natalie but each time I thought I could see her; my dreams frustratingly moved us to a different location, another unknown place. And then once again the search would start again in the same vain manner. I woke up, a little drained and knotted up inside. I drowned two cups of tea in quick succession in an attempt to shake this feeling off.

We set off just after nine am the following morning, the weather co-operating with sunshine. I had thought David would be quiet, subdued, anxious even. But it was like he was on serious caffeine overload, full of chatter and jokes. I found myself laughing at his warped humour as he re-countered his most memorable customers, my body unwinding and relaxing as I sped us along towards Cork.

David was just finishing a story about the lady in a feather hat wanting a hot strawberry frappe when I pulled in for a much welcome break at a roadside café.

'So what did you give her in the end?' I laughed as we climbed out, arching my aching back as I did. The roads in Ireland were not built for comfort, that was for sure. An hour here felt like two hours in reality, avoiding potholes, crazy drivers and traffic delays.

'Well now, I warmed some milk then added the strawberry sauce and called it my speciality frappe, created just for her. Worked like a charm.'

I pulled a face. 'Glorified warm milkshake …I don't think even your charm could sell me that.'

'Ah, so you do admit I have some charm then?' He grinned at me as he held open the door to the cafe. A whiff of coffee mixed into stale air greeted us as we walked in.

'Occasionally perhaps, though not used on any effective way on me.' My face was straight laced as I replied, though I inwardly smiled.

'Ouch! Cut deep why don't you, fiery?'

We sat down, nursing our lukewarm coffees we purchased at the less then clean counter. 'Now we're on the N22, we should be there in about an hour.' David commented

'Mm, famous last words. Does Ireland not do dual carriageways?' I grimaced, cranking my neck a little.

'What and spoil our lovely emerald isle that you tourists flock to admire?'

'I'm sure we would love it just as much with decent roads.'

'Thank you!' He planted a kiss on the startled girl's cheek, then spun in delight back to me. He grabbed my hand, nearly yanking my arm out of its joint in his excitement, and raced us back to the car.

I could hardly believe the turn of our good fortune. *Could this be it? Are we finally getting closer?* Were we right to be this breathless with anticipation?

Chapter Eleven

Hannah couldn't settle. She found herself pacing back and forth, her mind troubled.

All at once she turned sharply on her heel and hurried upstairs, heading straight to her pale lilac bedroom to open her wardrobe door. Her hand reached in to scramble around until, at last, she seized on what she had been searching for. Carefully, she pulled out an old faded shoebox.

As if it were made from sheer glass, Hannah carefully carried it over to the bed. Her hand shook a little as she slowly eased off the lid.

She reached down and pulled out two faded photos. The first was of her late husband, Lily's dad, taken the first time they went to Dingle. In fact, the first time they went on holiday outside of England. He was smiling, but there was something hidden in those eyes she hadn't seen at the time. Hannah closed her eyes with a sharp stabbing pain, and crumpling it a little, cast it to one side.

Then, taking a deep shaky breath, she reached in to tenderly take out the other photo, a snapshot frozen in time.

His eyes seem to bore deep into her, just as they always had the power to do. As she gazed at it, her eyes unexpectedly filled. Her finger stroked his features, before she looked away, breathing quickly. The photo remained tight in her clasp.

If Lily had been sitting beside her, she would have been stunned in silence - the likeness to his son was unmistakable.

David and I still sat in my car outside the girl's house, working out where this new address was. My phone began to ring. Not recognising the number, I answered with hesitation.

'Hello?'

'Lily? It's me, Greg!'

77

'Greg. Hi!' Came my surprised reply. My eyes inadvertently swung to David. His eyebrows shot up.

'Hope you don't mind me calling you out of the blue.'

'No, no that's fine.' I replied, puzzled as to how he came to have my number. As if reading my mind he cheerfully went on to explain.

'I badgered Ciara for your number. So now, listen, I have tonight off and I remembered you had promised me a drink on my next shift off. Can you do tonight?'

His confidence was a little unnerving and hard to say no to. I didn't exactly remember promising a drink with him, but with David looming silently beside me I felt rushed into making a reply.

'Oh, um … okay ... sure, I can meet you tonight. We should be back from Cork by then.' I questionably raised my eyebrows to David, seeking confirmation.

He gave a half shrug in reply, frowning a little. I pulled a face at him.

'Cork?! What the heck are you doing gracing that place?!'

'A good question. David and I are on a lead about this woman I'm looking for. '

'Oh, well now, tell me about it later. Pick you up about 7.30pm?'

'Okay, see you then. Bye.'

I dialled off, bemused and a tad off course. I felt David's eyes boring into me, surprising me with their intensity.

'Sorry about that.' I mumbled, feeling myself blush in mot a becoming way. Why did I feel a little guilty?

'You know we might not be back in time.' David answered a touch of haughtiness about his tone.

'Well, if we're not I'll call him to rearrange our … date.' I breezily replied, amazed at my laid back attitude. *Where had this girl sprung up from?!*

David gave a humph reply, muttering something dark under his breath. I let it pass, turning the engine on and pulling away from the side of the road.

'So where do I need to go?'

'Take a left up here.' His voice was still dark, edgy. There was silence for a moment, giving me time to ponder why David had suddenly turned into a petulant child. I had to admit, it was a little amusing. And a little exciting - o*h for crying out loud what was happening to me?! I don't have thoughts like that. Ever.*

'You know Greg has dated quite a few women recently.'

I swung my head round at that, mildly annoyed. 'That's entirely his business .. and mine, not yours. I thought he was a mate of yours anyway!'

'He is. I'm just warning you that's all. Hey, don't look at me like that! Just looking out for you, you know-'

'And why do you feel the sudden need to "look out for me"? Are you turning into some protective brother or because you're-' I just pulled back from saying "jealous" '- 'Oh blast! Now I've missed the turning because of you!!'

'For pity's sake, woman!'

After a few more tense moments, we finally got ourselves back on the right route, and about twenty minutes later were pulling up in another similar looking student style red bricked street.

I found myself holding my breath in anticipation as we went up the path. This time it felt different. This time Natalie could actually be living here. Even though she claimed it was her "friend's" address, it could well be a cover.

'Remember, be polite to this friend of your sister's.' I muttered. David shot me a dark look, but did pause to compose himself before knocking loudly on the door.

A long haired guy, in his late 20s, flung open the door, small headphones jammed into his pierced ears. On seeing us, he yanked one headphone out, with a not altogether friendly, 'Yes?'

David was eye balling the guy in return, looking a little threatening it had to be said. I groaned inwardly. *So much for my pet talk - one look at this guy and you don't like him. Is this what it was like having an older brother going all protective over nothing?*

I decided to step in, quick smart, before horns were locked and blood spilled over nothing. I gave my most winning smile and held out my hand to gain his attention. It worked, he finally broke the "stag about to do battle" stare with David and looked down at me, briefly taking my hand before he had realised what he was doing. His eyes warmed just a touch as I smiled wider.

'Hi, we're sorry to disturb you, but my friend here is looking for his sister, Natalie, and she has given us this address. Is she here at all?"

Slight stretch of the truth, but quick action was required.

He looked from one to the other of us, momentarily thrown. 'Natalie? No, sorry no-one by that name lives here.'

'Oh! Hold on..' I scrambled for the note with the address written on, almost sure there was a name with the address. Yes! 'What about .. Kim? Does she live here?'

The name, this time, had the desired impact. His face relaxed a little, despite he and David still being all edgy and bullish round each other. I ignored David, hoping this guy would do the same.

'Kim, yeah sure now, she's my girl. She's not here either. '

'Will she be back soon?'

He shook his head. 'No, she's on a shift at the restaurant she works at.'

I thought quickly. 'Oh, actually we're feeling a little hungry. Is it nearby?'

He indicated to the right with his head. 'Not far, no. Two roads up where you'll be finding it. Ricotta's.'

With that, he jammed his headphone back in, gave me a brief smile, David a brief glare, then shut the door in our face.

I didn't care. We had our next lead, and frankly that was all I cared about.

'Come on, stag.' I smiled, taking his hand firmly.

'What the hell are you talking about now?! And you know, I could have handled that back there!'

'Sure, sure. Hungry?'

Interesting choice of words "not far"... My feet were swollen to what felt like twice their normal size when we finally found the blasted place. The menu was starting to move over to early afternoon indulgence, rather than lunch, when we stumbled through its door. The sight of a seat had never looked more appealing. I'd almost lost sight of why we had been so determined to find this place.

David, on the other hand, had not. I was just reaching towards the table and the wonderful mercy of its seat, when I was aware David had shot off towards the bar at the back of the restaurant. Groaning, I dragged myself after him.

When I reached them, he was already chatting up the blond pretty girl making coffees. She was saying, while batting her eyelids in a very obvious way, 'Kim? She's just on a break at the moment. Why don't you have a coffee while you wait?'

I could have kissed her, quite literally, with gratitude. 'Fab plan.' I breathed out and without bothering to see if David was following me I collapsed onto the first seat I found near the bar.

The urge to take off my shoes was extreme, but I just managed to stop myself succumbing into temptation. Just.

David slid in opposite me.

'I've ordered some coffees.'

'And food?' I added hopefully, gazing at him so pitifully and for so long he finally slid back out and went back to the blond girl.

I felt an uncomfortable stab of jealousy as I watched them smiling and laughing as David leaned towards her over the bar. I forced myself to look away, and study the few lingering diners finishing off their late lunch special.

As I watched those around me, a little fascinated by their behaviour, their manners, and what brought them here, I heard my phone beep. I drew it out, saw I had one missed call from Nina, and one text from Mum. I opened the text "Hi its mum. Can you call me? Love me xxx"

'Two cheese paninis on their way.'

'Thanks.'

I slid the phone away without replying to the text, though my heart felt troubled by these messages from Mum. We never talked much about our feelings. What filled her heart and mind were both strangers to me; as mine were to her. What had caused this disturbance to our happy, comfy ways? Had I triggered it somehow by coming here? I sighed.

I looked up, to find David was watching me. 'You okay?'

I didn't even know how to begin explaining my confused feelings to him, when I couldn't get it straight in my mind. 'Just mum acting a little odd. Don't worry about it.' I added, smiling faintly.

Whatever comment David was about to say got swept away by the delicious smell of our cheese paninis arriving, melted cheese oozing out from the sides. It felt like manna from heaven. We hungrily tucked in.

'Hi, were you looking for me?'

Our heads swung up, our mouths full. A young, attractive slim girl with bottle red hair was smiling politely down at us. As her eyes connected with David, I heard a sharp intake of breath and I knew, right then, we had found Kim. There was no mistaking the similarity between brother and sister.

'Yes!' David half rose to meet her. 'I'm really hoping you can. I'm David … Natalie's brother. I.. I really need to find her, and I think you might know where she is.' His eyes held hers.

Kim stared at him. I could sense her shock at finding herself in this difficult position. There was a pause as we all eyed each other. Kim finally cleared her throat. 'Why do you think I know your sister?'

David gave her a pointed look, saying nothing. A flush appeared over her cheeks and I felt a little sorry for her, knowing David would give her no mercy till he got the answer he wanted.

'Okay, okay... then answer me this, why do you suddenly want to find her?' She had a defiant look in her eye now.

I saw an immense relief flood David's eyes as Kim acknowledged, albeit silently, that she did know Natalie.

'So she's alive...' He breathed out, his eyes briefly closing before reopening with shining brightness, excitement and pure physical joy touching their very depths. He turned and gave me the most beautiful hope-filled smile, his eyes dancing before me. I found my own smile break out in sheer delight and overwhelming relief.

Too driven now in getting this address and finally, *finally* seeing his sister, David ploughed on. 'Can you give me her address?'

Kim was already shaking her head, a little desperate shake, like she knew she couldn't fight against this strong current swamping her. 'Sorry, I can't. Don't ask me, okay? Look, maybe I could give her a call, ask her to call you or something.'

'No!' An explosive shout, startling us.

I stepped in, hoping to keep this calm. 'I know this is difficult for you, but please we really need your help-'

David cut through me, grabbing her arm without thinking. Kim tried to shake her arm free, her anger rising. The blond girl from behind the bar was starting to come towards us, a phone in her hand. Diners were stopping and staring at us.

'Let go of me!'

David released her. But his eyes were still frantic as Kim started to back away. 'Just leave her alone, she doesn't want to see you.'

'Let her tell me that for herself...' He went to follow her retreating back. 'Please! Help me! You're my only hope. I know she's in trouble-'

She froze then, turned to look back at him.

'Help me... ' David repeated, almost in a whisper.

Kim took one step towards us, frowning. I willed her closer still.

'Why do you think she's in trouble?' It was almost whispered out.

'She sent me a message, saying as much.' It was a slight bending of the truth but how else could David have explained it without alarming her further? 'Do you know where she is?'

Kim came right up to David now, as if challenging him in his sincerity. He held her gaze unwaveringly. No one could doubt the despair in his blue eyes. Kim gave a slight nod of her head, as if she knew then what she had to do.

'I can give you her address, but her number's not working at the moment ... I don't know why. Listen, she's not there much, at her flat, and she only works occasional shifts here.'

'When did you last see her?' I gently asked. I could see there was worry clouding her eyes as she hastily scribbled an address onto her order pad.

She briefly looked up at me. 'Three weeks or so, since she last worked a shift. I haven't had a text in a couple of days. It's not like her to be out of touch for that long, she usually calls or texts me every day.' She bit her lip.

'We'll find her.' I promised, sounding more certain then perhaps I felt.

Kim nodded, then reached out her hand to give the precious piece of paper to David.

He seized it, then her hands. 'Thank you. Thank you for trusting me with this. I can't tell you what this means.' He smiled, his eyes full of immense gratitude.

She nodded, her teeth still nibbling her lip. 'Tell her... tell her I'm thinking of her.'

'We will.'

With that, David took my arm and we walked out. I glanced back. Kim was still staring after us. Her waves of worry stretched out to swamp us.

Out of sight, David turned and suddenly grabbed me in his arms, spinning me round in delight. 'She's alive, Lily, my sister is alive!'

I laughed, tears springing into my eyes. 'I know! Thank you God...'

We both grinned sillily for another moment, our shared joy in this moment immeasurable, our joy unequal. Then he kissed me quickly on the cheek, before lowering me. We both stared at each other for a minute, before springing into action. There was no question of what that would be. As one, we sprinted back through the streets to my car, all fatigue fallen away; tiredness replaced with a high adrenaline rush.

As we finally fell into my car, David was already grabbing the map to search out the street.

'Wish you had a satnav.' He muttered.

'Cost too much as an extra.' I quipped back as I started the engine

We arrived outside a non-descript block of flats, quite new looking but basic, with no discerning character. The block of flats was one of many crammed into a too small space in this street in Cork. Ordinary place with ordinary people trying to earn a decent wage to keep their heads above water.

I turned to David. 'Ready?' I breathed.

He nodded, once, then climbed out of the car. I did likewise.

We came to an outer door, which should be closed but wasn't. Taking advantage of this golden opportunity, we bypassed the call system and went up the stairs to find number twenty two.

We now stood outside the blue slightly peeling door. My heart was beating fast. My mouth felt all dry and there's no way I could have said a word right then. Confronted with finally meeting her, I didn't know how to act or what to say. We were strangers ... yet her face had pulled me across hundreds of miles. She had radically altered my life in such a deep profound way, I couldn't even begin to comprehend this. *What should I say? How should I react ... And more importantly how would she react on seeing us?*

I stole a glance at David. His jaw was set firm, his thoughts private and contained. Looking straight ahead, he knocked loudly on the door.

The next few minutes seem to drag relentlessly, unforgiving. After a few minutes it was obvious Natalie was not home ... or choosing not to answer.

David, however, was fighting his own battle and was knocking once again, pounding as if his will and determination alone would magically let us in.

It was when he went to knock for the fifth time that I grabbed his arm to stop him.

'She's not in, David.' I said as gently as I could.

The anger in his eyes caused me to step back in surprise. He threw my hand off, then running agitated fingers through his hair, he abruptly pushed past me and disappeared.

When I finally caught up with him, he was pacing up and down the street outside. From the depths of him, he let out a roar that cut right through me. A flock of birds flew up in protest. In that moment, I felt totally helpless as I bore witness to his raw disappointment and acute frustration.

I came up to him, tried to soften the blow. 'We can come back and try again another day. Or maybe we could put a note through her door-'

'No, no, don't be stupid! That will just scare her away!'

I tried to hide my hurt at his condescending answer, telling myself he was hitting out in his frustration.

'Then we'll come back tom-

He was shaking his head, cutting me off. 'No, I'm staying put till I see her.' His face held a stubborn determination.

'That's crazy, she could be hours, or days even! You can't stay here all night. Be reasonable! We'll go home now, come back again. She 'll be here at some point!'

His pacing stopped, causing me to nearly collide with him. He towered over me. His face was twisted and totally unlike him. I hated that look on the spot.

'Sorry,' came his sarcastic reply, 'forgot you have your "date" to hurry back to. Please, don't let me stop you. Would hate to be an inconvenience to you. I don't need you now, anyway.'

It was like he had slapped me hard across the face, his words determined to deliver the greatest blow possible. I gasped in shock, stepping back, felt the burning of tears at the back of my throat. Anger against him hadn't quite come to the surface yet; instead vulnerability and self doubt swirled around inside me.

Blindly, I turned away from him, with no clear idea of where I was going. I angrily wiped away at my betraying tears. I saw my car and just headed for it, though the rational part of me knew I was in no condition to drive. But I didn't care, I just wanted to run away from this whole sorry scene... and from this sudden cold stranger.

I was just fumbling with my keys when a hand came out and grabbed me.

'Stop, wait. Lily.. Lily! .. Look at me!'

But I refused, still in vain trying to open my door, cursing my useless fingers under my breath.

'Lily, please! Stop that, let me apologise.' He half demanded, half pleaded. But I couldn't, wouldn't, let my feelings go so easily.

'No! Let me go, David!'

'Don't … I've acted like a complete asshole, taking it out on you. I'm sorry! Please.'

I knew if I met his eyes he would win me over. So instead I closed mine, stubbornly refusing to do his bidding.

'Asshole doesn't come close to it.' Came my bitter retort. 'How could you say that? Like I'm nothing more then someone to use, then dispose of ... like everything I've done for you means nothing-'

The sudden touch of his palm against my cold cheek, its gentleness making my skin tingle, made the rest of my words die away. He gently pulled my face round to his. His thumb absently wiped away a tear that had somehow escaped. Reluctantly, I raised my eyes to his. This time it was he who gasped a little on seeing the hurt clouding my eyes.

David lowered his forehead until it touched mine and we stayed like that for a moment.

'I'm sorry.' He said again, more humbly this time. 'I don't know what came over me. I didn't mean not needing you.' He laughed humourlessly. 'I need you more than ever. It was just … I thought I would see her, finally see her again and then.. then-' His voice broke, and with it my own hurt.

'Ssh, its okay.' I assured him, reaching up to place my hand over his which still cradled my cheek. 'Its okay, its forgotten. Remember, you promised me you wouldn't give up.' He nodded against me, drawing me tighter to him. 'We've come this far already. We're so close now to seeing her.'

He nodded again, allowing me to be a witness to his vulnerability. I pulled him into my arms, holding him as tight as I could. His head dropped onto my shoulder as his arms crushed me close.

We stayed like that until I felt strength surge back into him. Until my heart stopped fighting against the truth. Until there was nowhere else to hide from accepting my growing impossible love for him ...

Chapter Twelve

David offered to drive us home, and I was more than happy to let him. My body felt overwhelmingly tired and drained after everything that had happened today. My head was in a spin, and I could feel the beginnings of a headache pushing its way in.

I must have dozed off, because something made me jolt awake. As I struggled to focus and sit up, David lifted his hand away from where he'd briefly placed it on my shoulder.

'Sorry, I didn't know if to wake you or not, but thought you might like a coffee. I certainly do.'

He was rubbing his jaw. Dark shadows coated his eyes. The engine was turned off and we were parked outside a small, even more rundown service station to the one we stopped at earlier.

I hastily sat up straighter, discreetly attempting to smooth down my hair. 'Of course. Sorry, don't know why I fell asleep there… was I snoring?' I cringed.

David gave a short laugh. 'Well now, that wouldn't be very gentlemanly of me to comment on.'

'So in other words .. yes.' I groaned, embarrassed. I forced my weary self out of the car.

'We're not too far from home, less than an hour I'd say. Traffic slowed us down for a while, otherwise would have got you home and dry by now.' David commented, a wry note to his voice, as we sat down at a slightly cracked red seat, the table dubiously sticky; as I discovered when I had to prise my arm off it.

I nodded, while busy stirring sugar into my coffee. I glanced at my watch. Just after six. Possible to be back for 7.30pm to meet Greg… *though right now all I feel like doing is sinking deep into a hot, bubbly bath, glass of Rose in one hand, good book in the other, before falling into that all too soft bed waiting for me...*

I watched David grimace as he tasted the coffee. *Ever the café connoisseur*, I grinned to myself. Yet he had a point – this was grim stuff we were trying to drink here...

'So tell me how Cafe Peak came about.' I asked, daring to finally ask a more personal question.

He looked up, surprised, but was happy enough to fill in the details.

'I'd done a business management course at uni. Then when I left there, I decided to do a few courses in food hygiene, running your own business, coffee-making course,' Seeing my surprised look, David laughed, 'Yep, they even have courses for that! Anyway, I worked for a while in the kitchens of a couple of restaurants, which I detested, literally detested with a vengeance. I hated being stuck out back instead of at the front of the restaurant where I really wanted to be; meeting customers, being at the heart of the action. I dreamed about running my own cafe here, you know, of course I did, but didn't have the financial backing then.'

'So what changed?'

'Dad.' He said, simply. There was a faint smile to his face as he absently stirred his coffee. It was strangely mesmerising.

'He believed in me, gave me the backing I needed, with his blessing. Looking back now, I can see he already knew he was getting ill and wanted me to stop wandering from place to place, put down some roots. He could see this was the one thing, probably the only thing I was passionate about. Then, when he… passed away he made sure his Will provided enough for me to stay afloat in that first difficult year. And it was a hell of a difficult year.' He gave a short humourless laugh, shaking his head at the thought.

'He sounds pretty amazing, your dad.' I softly said.

'Ay, he was for sure. I still miss him.' His smile widened. 'But I know he would have been proud to see how well Cafe Peak is doing now.'

'Oh, without doubt!' I agreed. 'I love it in there. It's … a warm place to be. Somewhere you want to stay for a long time.' *Somewhere*

I wish I could always stay. With you. No, no, no Lily, stop that right now. You're scaring me.

David was staring at me, then he reached out to touch my hand. His eyes were grateful, touched. 'Thank you. That means a lot.'

I stared back, my mouth dry, my heart going all crazy thumping. Fear was creeping in to take a grip of me, so I quipped back more curtly then I meant to. 'I'm only saying this, of course, because you've promised me free cake.' David pulled back, letting go of my hand, giving me a strange smile. I felt a little foolish and so so stupid for letting my self doubt wreck this intimate moment.

After a silent moment, we made our way back to the car.

Before I knew it, or wanted, we were back in Dingle within the promised hour.

As David cut the engine in Ciara's driveway, we both turned to look at each other for a moment. I wanted to say oh I don't know something meaningful, but my mind had gone frustratingly blank. It was David who broke the silence.

'So... have a good evening. Tell him from me to treat you to the best on the menu.'

I nodded, still annoyingly tongue tied. 'Thanks.'

'Still okay to go back to Cork with me on Sunday? I can't leave Dora on her own tomorrow on our busiest day. Saturdays are crazy stupid there..'

'Yes, no, absolutely.' I managed to get out. *Why am I so reluctant to leave you?* Forcing myself to get a grip, I reached for my bag, hesitated for the briefest moment then leaned over and landed a quick kiss upon his rough cheek. My hair brushed against him as I slowly drew back. I caught the scent of his body spray, felt his hand almost reach out to touch me.

'I think I may need to get out too, seeing as this is your car.' He murmured. I could hear the laughter in his voice.

'Oh! Yes of course!' I stumbled out, feeling very stupid. *Oh how embarrassing...*

At last we were both out of the car. I locked it, trying to act normally, nonchalant... and not doing a very good job, to be honest.

'So okay bye then. See you Sunday.' I gave a quick brief wave then scuttled through into the sanctuary of Ciara's. I could see the shape of his shadow linger outside for a moment.... before moving away. I pressed my forehead against the cool wall, before finally walking upstairs.

Greg was surprisingly punctual for a man who gave the impression of being very laid back. I barely had time to change, apply some make up and brush out my hair, all the while giving the bath a lingering mournful look, before heading downstairs. I had planned to phone mum, but...

He gave me a kiss on the cheek, flashing me his cheeky grin, before escorting me by the arm down the road to "a grand little place I know".

I was pleasantly taken aback to find myself unwinding and relaxing in Greg's company, no doubt helped along by the constant refilling of my wine glass. I had managed to steer the conversation tactfully away from 'my search', concerned my tongue would run away from me and cause me to break confidence. Now we were on much safer ground. Greg was regaling to me stories of drinkers he had dealt with at his pub. I couldn't stop my laughter erupting, causing other diners to turn to look at us. I attempted to reign it in, but one look at Greg's comical expression as he choked on his wine, and that was all in vain.

'We're going to get thrown out at this rate!' I spluttered, wiping away tears.

'Ah, don't worry about that. The owner provides my food at the pub – so he wont want to be losing my business! More wine, girl!' Greg waved the almost empty bottle in front of me, a glee in his eyes.

'I seriously need to stop or you'll have to carry me back. And trust me, you're not strong enough for that.'

'You saying I'm not 'manly' enough to lift you over my shoulders?!'

'Well, if the cap fits...'

The conversation continued in this same vane; silly, comical, nonsensical. It was clear he was flirting with me, yet he didn't make me feel uncomfortable. Flattered maybe...

So I was very taken aback when Greg's face became more serious, quieter.

'Can't believe I didn't meet you a few weeks back when you first visited our emerald isle. Maybe I could have persuaded you to stay on...'

'Well, I'm not sure your powers of persuasion are that good!' I joked, laughing. Greg half smiled back, not returning my laughter. I swallowed back any further laughter and tried to adopt a more suitable serious expression. 'Well in fairness I mostly kept myself to myself and only stayed about four days.'

Greg nodded, took a sip of wine. 'Odd thing today.' He continued, 'I was telling my mum and dad about going out with you tonight. When I told them your name, mum abruptly walked out of the room without a word. ' Greg frowned, hard.

I leaned forward, my breath catching. 'Go on.' I encouraged.

'Then my dad seemed to go far off into his mind, like he completely forgot I was there for a long minute, before turning back to me and saying "I knew her mum, Hannah".'

'What?!' My voice was incredulous, shocked by this revelation. 'How do your parents know my mum? Did they know my dad too?'

Greg was shaking his head, hands spread apologetically. 'Sorry, I don't know, I couldn't get Dad to say anymore. He clammed up then, as if he regretted saying that much.' He paused. We both looked at each other, lost for words.

My mind was fumbled, slow after the wine, yet I had an unshakeable, strong feeling that this piece of information was of a huge vital importance to me. *But why? Why?*

'Didn't you say you came here as a kid?'

I nodded, absently playing with my dark red napkin as I tried to make sense of this.

'We did, but I thought for a holiday a couple of times, certainly not enough to get to know local people here. Maybe we stayed longer then I'd realised...'

Greg was silent for a moment, then touched my hand. My head swung up. His eyes were kind as he said, 'If you want to meet them to ask more, I'm sure I could get them to agree.'

I smiled appreciatively. 'Thank you.'

Greg seemed to pick up on my distraction, mingled with tiredness, and settled the bill. We walked back to Ciara's in the cool evening air, crisp with promised dew. He tucked my arm companionably into his and to be honest I was rather glad of the support back up the long wearisome hill.

As we reached the front door, I gave Greg a genuine warm smile. 'Thank you for such a great evening, I really enjoyed myself.'

'You sound surprised! But my pleasure, english lady. Come see me tomorrow and I'll give you the house special!' His grin was irresistible.

I laughed. 'I might just do that.'

Greg hesitated for the tiniest of seconds, then bent and gave me the briefest of kisses on the lips. It caught me unawares and before I had time to catch up, Greg was calling out goodbye and racing back down the hill at a fast, energetic pace.

Still feeling a little odd, I went in through the door and nearly gasped in shock when I noticed Ciara standing, as if frozen, at the bottom of the stairs. There was an odd look on her face that compelled me to say, 'Ciara! You made me jump! ... Are you okay?'

She seemed to give herself a shake, plastering on a more recognisable smile that did not quite reach her eyes. 'I'm sorry, I was just coming down the stairs when I saw you both, you know ...' Ciara gestured towards the door and I realised then she must have seen Greg kiss me.

'Oh! Yes…' I wasn't quite sure what to say and my voice trailed feebly off. I went to move towards the stairs. 'It's late, I should let you get on. Night, Ciara.'

'I hope you didn't mind me giving Greg your mobile number.' Her voice came out in a rush, stopping me. I turned back to her. She looked concerned, yes, but something more that I couldn't quite put my finger on. 'He can be very persistent, our Greg, when he wants to be. And, for sure, very determined and focussed. Passionate even. He wont do anything half heartedly, its all or nothing with him... and that includes relationships.'

I stared at her. She looked far away from me, in that moment. 'It sounds like you know him well.' I quietly commented, watching Ciara, silently wondering *how well? Am I treading on your toes?*

Ciara turned to me, half smiled. 'I do ... or did.'

One last word that told me profoundly more. So much sadness uttered behind it. Taken aback, my heart went out in pity to her. There was still more to be confided, I could feel that acutely. I wanted to gently encourage this, in this paused moment. But it was like someone suddenly switched a flip within her, for now she was all bright smiles, gently encouraging me 'to go to bed now, you must be tired.'

I found myself compiling with her wishes. And the moment was broken.

Chapter Thirteen

My feet felt laden, my mind subdued as I climbed the stairs to my room, mulling over first Ciara, then Greg, before finally resting on David.

I laid out on my bed after getting undressed, trying in vain to make sense of the last twenty four crazy hours. I don't think I've ever known a day like this, so full of emotional highs and lows, humour and pain, desire and dejection. And now a new dilemma; a dilemma so totally new and foreign to me that I had no idea how to handle it.

It was this. Two men had come storming into my life, who somehow were both finding space in my heart in different ways, when I'd thought no man had the ability to do that. Both were seemingly, somehow, unexplainably linked to my childhood, to my visits here with my family. One man was troubled, in need of my help, relying on my strength and perseverance. The other liked my company and could easily bring light heartedness and fun to my life, at least for a while, though by being with him I may be unintentionally bringing heartache to another women who didn't deserve it, if I was jumping to the right conclusions…

Such two contrasting strong men. Such two men, but only one heart of mine.

I'm so out of my comfort zone right now! And so confused. How should I be reacting to each of them? Am I leading one on, only to have to let him down later on? Am I hoping too much from the other, when I'll always be linked to this painful chapter of his life?

For reasons I refused to dwell on, I decided to avoid the café the following day. And though my feet itched to walk that way as I strolled along the harbour side, I stubbornly guided them away. I needed time to compose, regroup and for a short while still my confusing, conflicting thoughts. I basically wanted to feel like me again; content in my own company.

Earlier that morning I had tried to call mum. The phone had frustratingly gone to answer phone. I tapped my foot impatiently as I listened to her dulcet tones. 'Hi mum, its me. I'm still in Dingle. There's a .. couple of things I wanted to ask you about. Can you call me? Hope you're okay .. Bye.'

The restlessness had descended as soon as I'd hung up. There was something I should be seeing or working out – *it's right in front of my eyes, I know it is!* Yet for the life of me I couldn't see or understand what, or how, or why ...and that was *so* frustrating. Had there been more behind my brief childhood visits to Dingle? *Is this the reason I've been pulled here? Do I even dare to believe this is why Natalie called out to me – because she knew me from when we were young?* Yet ... yet David hadn't known me at all...

Unable to bear another minute of my constant maddening thoughts, I made the impulsive decision to head back to get my car. No question as to where I was heading. There was a murmur of rain in the sky overhead, but I didn't care.

I pointed the car in the direction of Inch beach.

It seemed I wasn't the only one daring to challenge the weather. There was quite a few people spread across its plain today, braving the sand as it quietly coated their clothes, idly chatting the hours away as they sipped from their steaming hot flask of coffee, or walking their exuberant dogs along its flat, reflective surface. The tide was far, far out to sea and the sand was enjoying the luxury of stretching out wide and beyond what my own limited vision could see.

I sat hugging my knees, watching the sea's constant steady movements, allowing it to relax and reassure me. I let the distant sound of the sea, as it caressed the sand, wash beautifully over me. The rain, when it came, was more refreshing then drenching.

I didn't pull out my camera. I didn't check my phone. I didn't try to think.

I existed in this moment…

Was simply here.

Later, my spirit refreshed and restored, I headed over to see Greg. With new determined resolve, I had decided to take up his offer of asking his parents to talk with me.

Gaelic noise was in its usual full flow as I pushed open the door. Warm air hit my frozen cheeks. Greg spotted me some way off and waved. His grin stretched across his face as I came near. Tell me, what girl wouldn't be flattered from the obvious delight on his face?

'Hello gorgeous.. you missed me, ah?'

I smiled as I perched on a stool by the bar. 'Perhaps I knew you would be missing me. . . Plus the promise of your house special was just too much to resist!'

'That I can understand, that I can! And I am a man of my word, just ask anyone here.' He nodded encouragingly for confirmation at two old crinkled weatherbeaten gentlemen sitting near me. They dutifully raised their pints in acknowledgement. One smiled at me, his face beautifully creased with age, his skin folded over like a parcel.

As I waited for my "special", I pulled out my phone out to check for messages. Nothing. *Typical!* Now when I wanted my mum to phone, she had gone frustratedly absent.

A sigh escaped unbridled. The crinkle faced man leaned a little closer. 'Don't worry, lass, he'll bring you something good.'

I laughed, despite. 'I'm sure he will.'

He winked then turned back to his drinking partner, tweaking his cap to me as he did.

'Here you go, one of my finest!' With a flourish, Greg put down a steaming plate of seafood before me. 'Freshly caught from our fine waters this very morning.'

'Wow it's … huge.' I managed to get out.

'Tuck in, don't be shy.'

'Okay.' I slowly replied, carefully picking up one of the prawns with my fork.

I made a "yumm" sound as I bit into its fleshy texture and, satisfied, he moved off to serve someone else.

Only then did I mercifully spit out the detested prawn into a napkin, nearly gagging as I did.

The crinkled man was watching me open mouthed now, laughing a little. I had the grace to look guilty. 'I don't like seafood.' I felt obliged to explain, then with sudden flash of quick inspired thinking I hastily pushed the plate towards them. 'Please, help me by eating this before Greg comes back! I don't want to hurt his feelings, but equally I will throw up all over this bar if I try to eat it.'

I gave them my most beseeching desperate look, while keeping half an eye on Greg; fortunately preoccupied for the moment.

The other man shrugged good naturedly. 'Never have been one to turn down free food. Pass it over then, love. '

With a grateful 'Thank you!' I did. I then watched with sheer amazement as they literally wolfed it down before sliding the plate back towards me. In the nick of time too; for Greg had reappeared beside us.

He looked amazed at my scraped clean plate. 'Impressive! Liked it then?'

I gave another non-committal "mmm" which seemed to appease him. The crinkly man burped rather loudly. We turned to stare at him. As I did, I noticed a telltale stain around his mouth and hastily distracted Greg before he connected the dots. 'Can I get some drinks for my two new friends over here?'

My 'two new friends' lit up with pleasure.

It was a little while later when I noticed David's friends, Amy and Sean, sitting alone in a corner. There was an intensity etched across their faces, and mannerisms that suggested "do not approach". It seemed Sean was trying to calm Amy down, his hand constantly going to touch her, though she kept shrugging him off.

He became aware of my gaze and looked over, flustering me. I gave a small hesitant smile accompanied by a slight wave. He returned it, but somehow the smile never reached his eyes, leaving me with a cold shivering feeling. Then Amy said something and he shifted his gaze back to her.

Frowning, I turned away. That feeling that something more was going on here, something connecting them to our search, came back stronger then ever as I sat sipping my drink. Only this time, it refused to be denied or pushed away.

This time it shouted at me loud and clear, and I couldn't shut it out.

Chapter Fourteen

We were hit by the inevitable 'déjà vu' as we once more headed back to Cork early sunday morning.

I was wishing with everything I possessed inside me that this wouldn't result in another soul-crushing wasted journey back…

I was aware of David casting glances towards me as I focused on the tricky narrow road ahead. Its effect was to make me feel very self conscious, so in the end I blurted out, 'Do I still have breakfast cereal round my mouth or something?' I threw a glance in his direction 'You keep looking at me without saying anything... it's a little unnerving to say the least.'

'Do I?' he replied in a mild, innocent tone. 'Perhaps I'm admiring your English rose complexion; so different from us ruddy locals.'

I gave him a withering look, yet felt a betraying blush spread across my cheeks. He gave a small laugh. I responded with a small punch to his arm.

'Ow! Do you mind?! Remind me not to compliment you again.' David muttered, rubbing the sore spot.

'I don't think you were complimenting me then!' I retorted, 'You were trying to evade answering my question.' I gave him a pointed look.

Still he evaded my question, fiddling now with my car stereo until a tune was pumping out of it. I became aware of his foot tapping on the car mat – in response to an underlying anxiousness or in natural rhythm to the music I really couldn't tell. Emeli Sande's powerful voice began to drift around us, and I found myself connecting in to her lyrics in a way I never had before.

Her song weaved itself around us, her words profound. Every sense in my body connected to her, straining to listen as she told me how the man you love may have given up, that no matter what they try to do it never feels enough, and its then, *then* you can show them a different kind of love, a new kind of love.

101

An intense feeling came over me, stilling me. My hands gripped the steering wheel. These words seem to cut straight into my heart, as if I had plucked them out from my very being to express all my deepest anguish and desire I was feeling for David... all that I hadn't, or couldn't, verbally say.

Her voice became louder; whether because of my own acute awareness of it or perhaps by David turning the volume up I had absolutely no idea; for I hadn't dared to look at him.

It was like she was singing about me. I had never been a party girl, hardly the one you go to for fun. But that meant nothing, not really. How you loved someone, how your heart beat for them – surely that was what defined you as a person?

I felt my own heart beat hard, fast. From the corner of my eye I saw David lean forward, turn his head a little towards me.

I will pick you up when you're crying, my heart yearned to tell him. *If you fall, I will reach out and grab you. Maybe that's the kind of love I can offer, when I never thought I was capable of offering anything to another.*

As I slowed the car down at a junction, I heard David gave a little intake of breath, felt his eyes fall on me once more. My breath quickened. I expelled it slowly, biting down on my lips. I was very aware something profound was happening within me, right here and now.

I dared to turn and look at him. The air felt static, as if it too was holding its breath. *This is my love, and I'm trying to offer it to you right now. Can you feel that, can you sense it? Do you even want me to fall for you?*

Our eyes locked and I could not look away, not for anything. I knew in that moment I was revealing everything stirring in my heart for this man, had laid myself bare before him. He didn't flinch away. But neither could I read his look.

A car honked loudly behind us, making us both physically jump. Flustered, I reeved off too fast, leaving a burning smell lingering after us.

The music moved on to a more upbeat tempo. We were both quiet. I felt confused, vulnerable, wanting David to break the silence first. I had never been one to make nervous conversation, found it irritating in others, I'm ashamed to admit. Yet now, as yesterday, I was struggling to not fall into that humiliating trap myself.

In fact my mouth was just opening to utter some insignificant comment when David became my unlikeliest saviour.

'How was your day yesterday?'

Though perhaps not giving me the most easiest of questions to answer.

'Um, good yes. I explored the area a little more, went back to Inch beach. It's so peaceful there, isn't it?'

David hesitated before answering. 'I think that you hold better thoughts with the beach then I do right now; taking everything into account.'

I looked across at him. 'But that might change for you.' I told him earnestly, 'It may give you the answer to your prayers.'

'Maybe.' he consented. 'So-o-o, had a good time with Greg friday night? Behaved himself, I hope.'

'Impeccably… mostly.'

An overwhelming urge to unburden my own family dilemmas gripped me. It felt like the most natural thing to do; share it with him. *But does he really want to hear my own problems? Does he care enough to listen?* I plunged in before I lost my nerve.

'Actually, Greg told me something about my own family that I don't really understand. Can I share it with you, see if you can shed a different light on it? Maybe help me make sense of it?'

'Course you can, Lil.' came his quick reassuring answer. I tried not to take too much pleasure from his intimate shortening of my name.

I began to tell him about all the odd comments and conversations I'd had since arriving, as well as my mum's complete 'out of character' reaction to my being here again.

'I feel like there's something so obvious staring me in the face, a piece of the puzzle, so to speak, which would explain everything. But I can't see it for the love of anything, and it's so maddening!'

'I know how that feels.' David commented wryly, 'And your mam's not given anything you can work with?'

I shook my head. 'No, and has gone from calling me constantly, to not returning any of my messages, and that in itself is so out of character for her! I've asked Greg if he can arrange for me to speak to his parents, but they could easily say no. I mean, all they know about me is my name and that's clearly not in my favour!'

I laughed without humour, then a thought flew into my mind. 'Mum reacted to your name! It's just come back to me. You don't remember me and my family do you, when we came to stay here? I know we would have all been kids at the time…'

David was already shaking his head. He looked over to me. 'Sorry, wish I could help but I don't remember you.' He paused then said, 'I know you're already lining up the mams, so to speak.' I laughed a little at this. 'But it seems like they're the missing piece you're talking about, just as you kept telling me for Nat. My own relationship with my mam may be strained of late, but we are still talking … just.' He added a little grimly. 'I can ask her what she knows, if you'd like.'

'Thank you.' I smiled gratefully. I unconsciously sighed, rubbing my forehead in a mildly agitated manner. 'It feels like there is a connection between us all; our parents, you, me, Greg, Natalie, with Dingle as the pulling thread. Its why or how that is leaving me empty handed right now. '

His hand fleetingly covered mine over the gear stick. I turned to him and caught his steady, confident look. 'We'll work this out. We will, you'll see.'

I nodded, smiling a little. 'Are you quoting me to me?' I quipped. David grinned.

A few moments later, he tensed up beside me as we gazed straight ahead .

'We're in Cork.' He quietly said.

A pulse quickened in her neck as Hannah picked up her abandoned phone. A guilty look swept over her at seeing the missed calls from her daughter. She bit her lip to try and stop the tremble quivering through her.

Closing her eyes for a moment, Hannah let out a long breath, then dialled the familiar number.

As it began to ring, Hannah was unable to sit still. She paced the room like a caged lioness.

Each ring seemed to draw itself out painfully.

It finally cut into Lily's answerphone. Was it relief or despair now brimming within Hannah's eyes?

I cursed out loud as I pulled sharply over to the edge of the road. David was already pulling my bag towards me from the back seat and I scrambled inside it trying to find my phone.

I had just seized it from the bottom of my bag pit and was pressing the accept call button, when it cut itself off. I cursed again. As I saw "missed call – mum" I dialled the number back. Engaged. As I disconnected, muttering loudly, it flashed up new voicemail. With a note of foreboding I pressed "listen now".

"Hi darling, sorry I keep missing your calls I've... been busy at work. Don't worry about calling back .. I've got to head off to .. a meeting. I'll call you later (*pause*) bye love."

'Oh for crying out loud!!'

My sense of frustration took me by surprise.

'Everything okay?'

I turned to David. His eyebrows were raised. The sight of my Cath Kidston flowery bag sitting on his lap made me smile despite my heightened tension.

'Sorry, just missed a call from mum. Don't worry, I'll call her later.'

'Sure now? I don't mind waiting.'

I shook my head, relieving him of my bag. 'It's fine.' I composed myself, refocusing. 'So do you want to go straight to the flat, or to the restaurant first to see if her friend Kim is there?'

He looked straight ahead. I could see his mind debating, rushing through the potential consequences of each action. I could only imagine how much was weighing upon him on this day, with the heavy knowledge of knowing his mum was anxiously waiting at home, unable to relax as she waited for news from her son of her daughter she had not seen in five long agonising years. I feverishly prayed I'd never experience that pain myself if I had children of my own – the constant throbbing pain of a missing child, nor the equally sharp pain of a child ostracised from you while he tried to deal with the betrayal of you hiding the truth from him.

Swallowing a rise of emotions, I reached out and grasped his hand. His fingers wrapped around mine almost to the point of pain.

I awaited his answer.

Now I waited for him, having watched his figure dart through the restaurant's doors.

My body was tense, alert. I felt something significant was about to take place. That today there could be no going back, no retreating to the ignorance of yesterday. Truth *would* be uncovered. I felt that keenly, a God given promise.

It felt like a lifetime waiting for him; the reality, of course, being only a few minutes. I straightened from leaning forward over the wheel as I finally saw him jog back through the summer rain to me. His face was unreadable as, head bent, David poured himself in. A rush of warm lingering rain filled the air around us.

'I saw Kim. She told me she'd had a text from Nat yesterday.'

'Thank God, that's great!' My face brightened on hearing this. 'Shall we try her flat again?'

David paused, turned to me. His face showed conflicting emotions, internal battles, a moment of insecurity.

'Now I might see her...' He began hesitantly, 'that it may be a reality.. I – I can't really explain this feeling in me, here .' He almost hit his chest. 'The loss of her has been .. immense. But what if – what if she wont-'

I stopped him by pressing my fingers against his lips, stilling the words before they were uttered. He stared at me. I gently shook my head, enjoying the sensation of my fingers against his parted lips. The tip of his tongue tingled my skin.

I reluctantly drew away, then smiled in encouragement. 'Ready?'

David let out a long ragged breath..

The door seemed to loom large before us, a solid wall that had the power to refuse us entry. We knocked on the door. Trepidation seized me.

Expecting to turn away disappointed from no reply, when it instead swung open I couldn't quite keep up with this new turn of events. Dazzling light from the hallway wrapped itself around us.

David took an eager step forward. He was ready to play for real now this scene he had rehearsed so frequently in his mind.

So when a stranger's face stood there giving us an inquisitive yet cautious smile, neither of us could utter a word for a moment; so sharp was this knife of disappointment.

'Can I help you?' The stranger was looking at us. She was young, soft in features, dressed casually in jeans and a stripy top, giving off a pleasant demeanour.

But she was not Natalie.

I turned in despair to David. He was staring at this girl as if willing her to physically change before our very eyes.

'I'm sorry –' I began, not really sure what I was going to apologise for.

'Where's Nat?' David stuttered out, despair edging his voice. 'I was told she lived here .. where's my-?'

I was trying to pull him away, knowing this was fruitless questioning. The young woman was looking wild eyed at him and I didn't want us to alarm her.

'Its okay, come on David.' I gently urged, cutting him off. 'Sorry, we were looking for someone-'

'Gill, who is it?'

A girl of around 4 or 5 pushed her way round the door and now stood staring up at us. Her big blue eyes locked onto David. There was a quizzical look on her face as she gazed up at him. He stared at her without really seeing her. Before the woman had time to respond, the dark haired girl had ran off again.

I gently took David's arm to encourage him to go, but his feet were frozen to the spot, as if his entire body was rebelling against this bitter truth.

'Sorry about Lottie, who were you looking for again?' The woman was giving David a sympathetic look.

Then all at once something changed in her demeanour. She gave a sudden sharp inhale.

I stared at her. She stared at David.

Lottie appeared, grasping something in her hands. I think it was a photo. She reached out and pulled on David's arm. He slowly dragged his eyes down to her. She grinned up at him, revealing a missing tooth as she did.

'Uncle David!'

Every breath and particle froze around us, within us, before us.

Chapter Fifteen

If you had asked me later what exactly was said in those defining moments afterwards, as we all stood locked together in that dusky, damp hallway, I honestly could not have told you.

What I do remember is that full paralysing moment when the world seemed to rock on its axle.... then of everyone talking at once. I remember David staring down in stunned and utter shock at this niece he had known nothing about, before asking, in a remarkably restrained voice, if he could look at the photo she grasped. I can still see Lottie obliging; but looking a little frightened now by our reaction. I remember her nanny bending down to hug her; Lottie beginning to cry and we being asked, politely but firmly, to come back tomorrow when Natalie would be home.

I remember catching the barest of glances at the sepia photo – that of a smiling David and Nat – before David reluctantly handed it back. And I know that I will never forget having to drag him away; when every fibre within him screamed and rebelled against me.

There was a shell shocked look about him as we stumbled away. I folded him into the car and pulled away as fast as I could.

I raced us for home, breaking every Irish speed limit as I did. I didn't try to engage him in conversation with inane remarks. And I didn't try to make this right for him. How could I? What could I possibly say to make this all okay and normal? I just wanted to eat up the miles as quickly as I dared. I barely noticed the passing scenery as my mind raged an internal battle.

The truth, the brutal truth was, I felt totally unprepared for this revelation. And I wanted to run. So far. As far away as I possibly could. My natural switch to hide away from emotions, and precisely these kind of confrontations, was pushing its ugly way up to the surface. How could I possibly explain or excuse this new discovered secret of four year old Lottie, when I felt completely repelled by this constant dishonesty within his family?

I don't know what to do!! Tears pricked the back of my eyes. I forced them back, swallowing hard against the ache at the back of my throat. I knew it made no sense; to be this upset. For crying out loud! *Its not like this latest betrayal had been committed against me.* Is this what feels like to love someone – to feel their pain like its your own? If so, then maybe I'm not strong enough -

You're strong enough.

The words jumped strongly and clearly into my mind, as if from nowhere. I think I must have gasped a little. In that same moment, I felt a surge of strength fill my limbs, my resolve, my very being. Calmness gently washed over me. I wanted to drink it all in, be transformed by it. Be thankful for it.

The next moment I saw a sign for Iona beach. And I knew then exactly what to do...

As I pulled up and turned the engine off, David slowly became aware of our surroundings. Frowning, he stared ahead at the beach.

'Why have we stopped here? I don't want to be here-'

I was already out of the car and round to his side. I opened his door and practically pulled him out.

'Come with me.'

I could sense David reticence and barely controlled anger as he stumbled after me. But I had the sixth sense to know it wasn't directed at me ... yet neither was it about to disappear like misty vapour. I resolutely took hold of his arm, determined not to waiver.

'What the hell are you doing, Lil?! You think I fancy some nice and cosy walk along the beach? I don't - especially this one... I loath this one!'

'No, you don't.' I said firmly, not letting go for an instant as our heavy footprints left their mark in the wet sand.

'Don't talk to me like some flippin' eejit!'

'Then quit acting like one! You don't like what it represents, that's all. It's not this beach's fault.'

David stopped without warning, his eyes blazing in anger and nearly toppling us both over with the force of it. 'If anything its tried to help you!' I stormed on.

'Don't give me that crap mystical nonsense! Now are you going to drive me home or do I need to walk?! So help me, God...'

David had already began to stumble across the sand. The rational part of me was saying *"let him go!"*. But this new determined part of me just couldn't.

I nearly stumbled over in my haste to get in front of him, my feet weighed down by the restricting gluelike sand. Somehow I grabbed his arm and held on grimly.

'Are you just going to run away from your anger and hurt and pain and everything else that you're feeling right now?! Is that it? Is that your glorious plan?'

'Maybe that's exactly what I'm going to do, it seems to be what my family do best-'

'It doesn't have to be what you do, don't you see?! Rant and rave and scream out loud against the unfairness of it all. If anyone deserves to, you do! Don't tell me you're not angry at your sister for keeping this child a secret? Look at me... *look at me! Tell me!*'

David's eye were ablaze by now, almost wild. 'You want to know?! I'll tell you ... I feel sick, physically sick in here.' He jabbed at his chest. 'Wherever I look, whatever I do every time thinking there can't be any more secrets or lies I find out more! And I hate it, *I hate it!* Because now I don't even know my own family ... its like they've become strangers! No, worse than strangers!'

All at once, his face crumpled, like someone or something had whooshed right through him and whipped away all the anger, leaving him with only the pain and no way to vent it out. His hands grabbed roughly at his hair. His voice held a broken note. 'I don't want to know anymore. I ... I cant do this -'

I was reaching out, trying to still his hands. 'Shh, its okay, it's okay, David.'

Instinctively I stepped closer still until our bodies were almost touching. My hands came up to cradle his face, my mouth pressed little kisses onto his cheeks until I reached his mouth. Before I allowed myself to think, I let my mouth press against his, drawing him into a kiss.

For a moment, he was still against me. Then I felt him respond, pull me up against him and we were kissing with an almost desperation, the emotions of the last day giving this moment a heightened intensity. It felt so natural, so right, and it took all my willpower to finally pull my mouth away from his.

We stared at each other for a moment, trying to gain our breath. *What have I just done?! Who is this passionate girl?* Then David gave a small short laugh as he shook his head. 'Well that was better than a slap, and no kidding.'

I found myself half laughing, half crying. David dropped his head against mine, his breathing a little erratic. 'Thank you.' he whispered.

'My pleasure.' I whispered back.

We stood for a moment like that, holding tight, then David pressed his lips against my cheek and then down to my neck. I closed my eyes, enjoying the sensation as he gathered me close.

'Mind if I take the lead this time?'

My heart sung. 'Not at all.' I murmured against his smile, before we kissed once more.

He sees me, at last he sees me!

Have you ever wanted to freeze frame a moment and let nothing enter in or come out; not even a single particle of golden sand? To see this clear, beautiful picture of how your life could be, and want to press pause and soak it in? Just absorb every colour, flavour and taste of it? Then replay it again and again...

Because you know this precious gift that's taken you by surprise and delight and joy, is here but for a breathtaking moment before normal life crashes in, the play button pressed once more and the world comes crashing back in. That's the way of life; golden light moments that fill you with delight, and can be grasped close to your heart to help you through the darker moments of this world.

112

Oh, I felt this so acutely, so intensely, right now, and it only seemed to heighten every emotion this evening with David. I somehow knew to grab on to its memory, its gift, before I would lose him again. For of course I would; lose him. I couldn't be his priority, the one uppermost in his thoughts and feelings ... too many others were already cramming for that space.

But I did have him right now. And would till morning at least. That was enough for me.

We sat long into the evening on Inch Beach, watching the calming waves, talking softly as we pressed close to each other, kissing, exploring the feel of each other's face, mouth, hands, neck... And with every touch and every kiss an intensity was building, a desire and need for more. He felt it as strongly as I did; his eyes were hiding nothing from me and I rejoiced in it, felt insanely happy and giddy at this new intimate feeling of closeness to another being. It was addictive and crazy and a small part of me was already mourning this discovery. *How am I ever going to go back to how I was before; all locked away?*

Coldness and hunger finally forced us to leave, as the last stunning red rays of sunlight finally gave way to the growing darkness. We laughed as we stumbled across the sand, barely seeing where we were going, pulling each other out of the sticky sand. David nearly lost a shoe at one point, and we both toppled over, hysterical, as we tried to pull it out of the resisting sand. We finally got to my car, coated in wet sand that was already itching me under my clothes. When David said, 'I think you need one of my famous coffee and fruit toast.' I grinned, leaned forward as if to kiss him, only to at the last moment shove wet sand down his neck from where I'd had hidden some in my hand.

He gave a girlie scream. 'AAH! That's horrible, get it out! Get it out! Oh, you will pay for that, fiery!' With that, David grabbed an hysterical me.

'Promises, promises...'

It was some time before we finally drove off...

Now we sat cosied up in his cafe, warming our hands around our steaming coffees, the plate between us empty now apart from a few abandoned crumbs and trickling melted butter.

David was gazing at me. His lips were parted into a peaceful smile, his eyes relaxed and warm in a way I'd never seen before. I knew I'd done that and this, more than anything, made me feel I had a sole purpose and reason in being here, in this exact moment, with him. My love for him wouldn't be wasted or rejected. At least not tonight...

'You know you're not allowed to leave here now. You have to stay here with me, sipping coffee, for as long as I say. And that's the God honest truth, so there's no point in coming up with a counter defensive...'

I raised my eyebrows, feigning protest when inside I wanted to give a very loud and undignified whoop.

'So is that what you Irish men do, then? Keep us english girls locked up here on your shores until we are... seduced or something?!'

He leaned in, grinning as he stroked my cheek. 'We are known, of course, for being great seducers … And if that fails, then we just take away your passport.' He shrugged nonchalantly.

I leaned closer still, so we could almost feel the other's breath. My fingers touched his lips as I murmured. 'Except now you've told me your tactics, I will be immune to them.'

I gasped as he gently nibbled my fingertip. 'So sure you are immune? Because I have a feeling you're ripe for seduction.'

Before I had a chance to protest at his outrageous confidence he pulled my mouth to his, his fingers caressing my neck, before threading their way through my hair. I closed my eyes and gave myself up to the moment, enjoying the touch of him, the sensation of letting my tight constraints be so tenderly released.

I moved off my chair, frustrated as he was by the table, and he tugged me down onto his lap as we barely paused in kissing. At last I could hold him tight, my hand moving from his face down to his chest. His mouth moved to my neck, his hands travelling down my body, and my head bent back as I closed my eyes.

Vaguely I was aware of the cafe door opening, of footsteps approaching, but couldn't nor wanted to break away from David, from this incredible moment. It seemed David felt the same for without letting go, he broke away enough to shout, 'We're closed!' before going to kiss me again.

Yet whoever it was seemed determined to remain. No faint sound of the door, which we'd forgotten to lock, re-closing again. This time we both lifted our heads, full of pent up frustration. I felt the unstoppable threads of reality trying to reclaim us, even though every fibre in me was ready to battle against it.

'I said we're- ' David suddenly stopped as he properly focused on the person standing there. He half stood and I had no choice but to stand up too, look properly at this person who dared to interrupt us with their rights more important than our own.

As I stared at her, her dark wavy locks pulled back into a ponytail, her eyes ignoring me as she focused all her energy and courage on David, I stepped back in shock.

She took one step closer. 'Davie?'

I turned to look at him. He was swallowing hard, a constant changing tide of emotions sweeping his features. Then he said hesitantly, as if to actually say her name out loud might make her vanish again. 'Nat?'

With that she was nodding, letting out a cry, 'Yes! Yes, its me.' Nat rushed over and threw herself into her brother's arms. For a moment David stood there stunned, then he was hugging her back, a joyful cry escaping from him as they held each other tight. 'Thank God, thank God, you're back.' He half sobbed into her hair.

I watched them for a moment, overcome with tears myself. I took one step back, then another, not wanting to intrude. As I gazed at them, I tried to ignore this rising tide of despair and rejection burning within me, to tell myself to stop being so selfish, to just be happy for David...

But it came over me anyway, and I couldn't seem to fight it. The room began to feel unreal, like I was watching this from far away.

This was what we'd been dreaming of - finding his sister. And I'd been a big part of this journey. It was, without a doubt, amazing, incredible. A miracle even.

But I also knew, with utter clarity, that my part in their lives may just have come to an end, his reliance on me; no more. I would be an easy character to write out of this story now. And I had no say in any of it.

He finally saw me! He touched me, let me touch a deeper part of him... Yet why do I now fear that this need for me is going to dim, fade away... I'm going to lose him before I ever really had him.

I knew I only had tonight. But couldn't I have been given just a few more hours? Just a little more time to freeze frame, before the play button was hit again?

Chapter Sixteen

It was Natalie who was the first to let go, take a step back, glance over to me as she did. It was difficult to say who felt the more awkward ... but feared it was probably me; after all I was hardly a dot on her radar right then.

It did however mean that David suddenly remembered my presence and quickly took a step towards me, grabbing my hand to pull me towards his sister. It was clear in his eyes he had already forgiven his sister for breaking their hearts in leaving them, and in doing so conceal the existence of her daughter. Once again I was taken aback by his generous nature, though I was filled with concern at this easy acceptance.

His voice was ecstatic, incredible, heightened by emotion. 'Lil, come and meet my sister, Nat! Nat, this is Lily; you won't believe how much she's been a part of you coming back.' He dropped my hand before I could say anything; to hug his now laughing sister again. 'I can't believe you're here! It's just-'

'I know, I know ... we have so much to talk about.'

Natalie glanced over at me again, a cautious smile on her face. Our eyes locked for a moment as I saw a thousand questions flash through her eyes. I found my voice enough to say, 'It's so good to finally meet you, Natalie. This is just amazing ... just incredible...David has wanted this...'

I trailed off, uncertain of where I was going with this. What did you say in this kind of situation? That we have given every moment to this, had shed tears over, in fact put our own lives on hold for you.

And there was so many questions I wanted to ask – none more pressing than '*Why was it me you appeared to?*'

I mean, come on, do we know each other? Or have known each other in the past? *Do you have any idea how much you've hurt your family, your brother? Give me some answers please!*

But how could I say any of this? Of course I can't. All I could do was stare stupidly at this woman who up till now had lived only in my photo, her face imprinted on what felt like my very soul, who now stood here, in the flesh, staring curiously back at me.

And not one chord of despair etched across her face! Where was it, because I swear to God that was the only thing that had pulled me to her.

Instead all I saw, as she turned her head away from me, almost dismissing me from their presence – was selfishness. And that shocked me to the core, because I wasn't prepared for that. I had been expecting a woman in desperate need ... but Natalie did not appear to be a woman who needed any help, certainly not for me.

Anger and pain contracted sharply within me, but I forced them back down.

David was smiling absently at me but his mind was elsewhere, working furiously. He turned to Natalie. 'Have you seen mam yet? She's going to be stoked-'

Natalie was shaking her head, stilling him. 'Not yet .. I needed to come to you first. Do you think we can just talk for a while?' Her eyes pleaded with his.

David was already nodding. 'Of course, of course we can. . let me lock up here so we can go up to my flat.'

He turned to me, freezing for a moment, hesitating. I waited for a tantalising, excruciating moment hoping.. for I don't know what. But it became painfully clear I was the unwanted one here, so forced a smile to my lips. 'Don't worry I'll lock up and post the keys back through the letterbox. You two go. I'll .. see you tomorrow maybe?'

He came up to me, looked deep into my eyes for one beautiful moment. 'Thank you, Lil. Thanks for everything.' His keys, cold to the touch, were pressed into my hand.

I felt his lips briefly on my cheek; touching my cool skin. Then they were gone, taking with it their warmth. I stood there suspended, unable to motivate myself to move or react.

And all I could keep asking myself again and again were four simple but tormenting words...

118

Was that his goodbye?

Now I stood at the furthest point of the pier, staring hard into the darkness as if I could will it into giving me the answers I desperately sought. I felt shivery, inside and out, but refused to give my body any relief by going inside to the warmth, even though every bone ached.

I knew tomorrow I would have to face reality. I didn't have any more reason for staying here; except to seek answers for my own peace of mind. Natalie didn't need me, that much was clear, and I couldn't even begin to process what was my reason for coming here was. It was too soul destroying.

I had to face the fact that come tomorrow, practical details would need to be sorted for returning home – though, right now, "home" felt more of a stranger to me then here, in this beautiful south west point of Ireland.

But tonight .. tonight I will allow myself the luxury of reliving his touch, his embrace. Tonight I will allow myself to cry just a little, to wallow some, my heart to ache freely. I'm not going to fight back against this rising tide of pain building up inside me.

I let my eyes slowly close.

From the enveloping darkness came sudden footsteps behind me and for a brief tantalising moment I thought 'He's come back!' I spun round, a smile already lighting up my face … only to have it fade limply away when I saw it was Greg, staring bemusedly at me.

'Lily? What are you doing out here ... you look frozen to the core, that you do! I saw you as I was leaving my pub and thought "I recognise that brunette head". Come on; let me take you back to Ciara's, get you warmed up.'

He was already taking my hand and somehow I didn't have to energy to fight it. I allowed myself to be taken away, lean a little into his strength, let his amiable words soothe and wash over me. He didn't seem to worry if I answered him or not ... and for that I was grateful.

The morning came at last, sweeping away the darkness. I slowly crawled out of bed and padded over to the window, wrapping my dressing gown tightly around me. I gazed down over the chimney pots, hoping the calmness of this constant view would settle me down, focus my mind. It worked a little.

My phone beeped behind me, signalling a text arriving. I spun around and grabbed it, hoping beyond hope it was from David, wanting desperately to speak to him.

Greg's name flashed up on my screen. Acute disappointment flooded me. I opened the text nonetheless.

"Just wanted 2 check ur ok…! Call me."

I closed it without replying, telling myself I would later.

After breakfast, in a bid to try and shift away this lethargy pressing down on me, and to resist checking my phone every five minutes to the point of going insane, I opened my laptop and began to write a few emails. The first was to my boss; confirmation I would be returning next week (if I still had my job), and second to Nina to tell her the same. I tried to compose an email to mum, but failed miserably. I would call her later. I was just reluctantly looking at flights online to London Gatwick when my phone rang. I leapt up to get it, knocking over my mug of tea in my clumsy haste.

"Greg calling" flashed up.

I let out a short shout of frustration, hesitated for a moment then pressed "accept".

My voice was apologetic. 'Hi Greg. Sorry I've not called you back yet.'

'So now you don't sound like you're dying from hyperthermia, so that's a bonus.'

I smiled despite myself. 'No, I'm made of tough stuff really ... for an English girl.'

'I didn't like to say, but you know what they say about mad dogs and englishmen .. feeling may be more than a little appropriate in your case. You certainly wouldn't catch any of us locals standing out there till we're completely brass monkeys, that I can tell you!'

I laughed, feeling lighter of spirit. There was a slight pause his end then, 'Are you around later to meet up?'

I need to tell him the truth. 'Actually that would be good, I do need to chat with you. '

'Me too. Want to come round later when it's a little quieter at the pub?'

'Sure, around three okay?'

We said goodbye. I pressed the phone to my mouth, my mind already trying hard to form the right words. I didn't want to lead him on or give false hope, when right now all I could think and feel was David. Plus I still couldn't shake the feeling there was more under the surface between Ciara and him. Greg was great, without doubt, but maybe his 'greatness' was meant to shine on to someone else … someone like Ciara. I really wanted to gently probe them further …but maybe when my head was a little clearer.

Time dragged on painfully. I had come up with every excuse under the sun for not booking my flight; it's amazing how persuasive I could be when I really tried. But putting off the inevitable is precisely that … inevitable. I finally confirmed the reservation for two days time, late flight.

Still there was no word from David. Of course there wasn't.

At last the hour crept round to three pm. Although I was reluctant to have this conversation, and tell Greg that we could never be anything more than friends, at least I would have some human contact. Ciara had been busy all day, with no time to chat, though clearly she wanted to as much as I did. And today, today I was my own worse enemy. I didn't want to be me, I didn't want to be this girl today. The girl from yesterday evening; that's who I wanted to be.

My two old friends from the other night were sitting in their usual spots, in easy reach of the bar. I smiled warmly, waving at them as I walked over to the bar. They tipped their pint glasses at me, their lined faces crinkling up.

Greg's back was to me as I approached and so I called out a soft, 'Hello'.

He turned around, and a smile spread across his face.

'Well now, you certainly don't look ill in any way. In fact, quite gorgeous!'

I blushed, a little taken aback. Was it wrong to enjoy this compliment? 'I'm not sure that's entirely true ...'

'Learn to take a compliment, Lily. '

'Okay ... I'll try. Thank you. So, I guess we should have that chat?' *Before I lose my bottle and be swept away by your very easy charm...*

Greg looked at his watch, then was all of a sudden all action. 'We're chat on our way over. Pete, over here!'

I looked at him in bewilderment as he started issuing orders to his bartender. 'Go where?!'

I was talking to thin air. I threw up my hands, aware of chuckling coming from the direction of my two old friends. I gave them a helpless shrug. Greg reappeared at this point, coat being slung on as he walked around to my side.

'Let's go!'

'Greg! I repeat, go where?!!'

He stopped and looked at me like it was obvious. 'To see my Dad of course, like you asked. He wants to meet you.' With that he started heading to the door.

I stared in shock at his retreating back, before hurrying after him.

We pulled up outside a fairly modern looking detached bungalow, a mixture of stonewash and brick. It was plain to see it was quite an expensive place. I could see from the large bay windows at the front and rear that you could drink up some impressive views over the Dingle peninsular from all sides of this bungalow.

Before I had time to draw breath, I found myself sitting opposite a gentle looking man, slightly faded in age but still holding something strong in his eyes, with softly waving white hair. There was a striking family likeness between father and son– the same easy smile, those speckled hazel eyes, the same broad shoulders. It was quite staggering, and I had to stop myself gasping out loud. It was like they were one.

Greg made the introductions, and I found myself shaking hands with Edward, Ted for short. He held my hand for longer than considered polite, but I didn't feel affronted. At last Ted gave me a smile, looked over to Greg and gently but firmly shooed him out of the room on the pretence of making us all a pot of tea. There was no sign of Greg's mum and I felt it was too presumptuous to ask where she was.

'I understand you wanted to know about my knowing your mam?' Ted began with no preamble, his voice eager, the accent heightened. 'Is your mam … is Hannah ... here with you?'

I was quick to shake my head. 'No, just me. I felt a... pull here.'

'Dingle can do that to you.' His voice had lost a spark from a moment ago, I noticed.

I waited patiently, though every part of me strained to force this conversation forward. I knew I was stepping on a rocky uneven surface that could trip me up, cause pain and discomfort. Now it was my time to feel how David must have felt for the last two weeks – to know a little but still be so unprepared for the bare, perhaps brutal, truth. Two weeks ago I'd been naïve, barely giving my mum and her past any thought, her feelings and desires mostly disregarded by me. Not so much in a cruel way, but in a way all children did when it came to their own parents.

Ted sat back, broke his gaze from me to stare unseeing out of the large bay window dominating one side.

'I remember you as a wee girl, about eight or thereabouts. You came here to our house, were a shy little thing. It took some persuasion to get you to play with Greg.'

I cleared my throat, had to ask, 'Do you mean when we came here on holiday; as a family?'

123

He turned to look at me, paused for so long I began to wonder if he hadn't heard. A conflicting emotion clouded his face before Ted quietly said, 'Lily, you lived in Dingle for three months. Do you not remember?'

I gasped. 'Three months?! Are you sure?' I shook my head. 'I don't remember it very well, just the vaguest feeling of knowing this place. Mum never said...' I stopped, tried to gather my thoughts coherently. 'But Dad couldn't have taken that long off, surely?'

A look of sympathy, then, 'Your pa wasn't with you, love.'

I stared at him, unconsciously moving forward on the sofa. I felt confused, a little disorientated. How could he have not been with us? Where was he? Surely I would remember this, even though I was young? 'I don't understand.' I half whispered.

I began to feel a weight pressing down on me, making it hard to breathe. I fought the childish urge to run out of here before he could tell me anymore.

It was as if he read my mind. 'I can't tell you more than that, it's not my place.' Ted was leaning forward himself now, an urgency about him I couldn't fail to respond to. 'You must talk to your mam.' He further pressed.

I gave a brief nod, which he seemed satisfied with. Again the silence, again unable to stop myself from breaking it. 'Excuse me for my bluntness, but I'm trying to understand how you fit into all this..'

This time the pause was deafening, before -

'I fell for her... I fell for your mam while I was trying to help her.'

The words hung suspended, captured by the floating particles. I didn't know what to say or how to react, completely stunned into silence. 'Fell for her?' I stupidly repeated

He looked kindly at me. 'Yes. And her for me.'

'You mean you had an … affair?' The word felt wrong on my lips, as if saying it was a betrayal to my mum.

Ted shook his head. Relief flooded me. 'No, at least not in the traditional sense. We never let ourselves start anything ... physical. We hadn't dared.'

Before I could say anymore, he hurried on, his voice thick with emotion and that sense of urgency again.

'Lily, you may be too young to have experienced this. You may not be married, so never experienced how a love between a married couple can slowly die away from not being protected or nurtured enough. Then a woman comes along, needing a friend, needing a shoulder to lean on and first of all your thoughts are innocent, you just want to help her. You draw naturally closer to each other. One innocent touch later, a meeting of eyes and then you no longer see her as a friend ... you see her as a woman, and she sees you as a man. Strong emotions and desire are evoked.... And then everything changes. That's what happened to us. I should have walked away, but I couldn't. I didn't want to. Perhaps I was too weak, too desperate. We knew we had to say goodbye at some point and she was the stronger one in the end. The day she left - something broke in me.'

Ted's eyes locked intensely with mine. 'I hope you never have to feel pain like that. It never completely leaves you. Hannah has never left me... in here.' His hand pressed down almost brutally over his heart. His eyes dared me to challenge him.

But the pain disturbing the pupils of those eyes left me in no doubt of the truth.

He loved her still. He loved my mum.

And now he'd given me the burden of knowing this too.

Chapter Seventeen

It would have been impossible for Greg not to pick up on the somewhat strained atmosphere between his father and I when he walked back in, carrying a tray bearing a steaming teapot, milk jug, dainty teacups and plate of bourbon biscuits.

Ted and I exchanged a silent intense look. Yet there was no fear on his face that I would reveal the truth to his son – which meant he either didn't care if it did come out... or trusted me without doubt because of whose daughter I was.

I struggled to know what to say to this man; a stranger to me ... yet an intimate friend, lover or whatever you call him to my mum. I felt like bolting out of the room, and pretend I hadn't heard what I just had. I wanted to erase it from my memory because I had no idea what to do with this. I wanted to run to David and pour it all out to him. I wanted to scream at my mum for this betrayal to my dad.

All of this was swirling wildly around my head. But I bit down hard against it, slipped back into the polite, well mannered girl I'd been brought up to be. I drank my tea as fast as I could though it scalded my throat, and swallowed down, without really tasting, the proffered bourbon. Then as quick as politeness allowed, I made my excuses.

As I stood, Ted sprang up, took my cold hand in his. His eyes pleaded with mine. 'Please, pass on my regards to your mam. Tell her... tell her I hope she is happy.'

I felt his sadness wash over me. I swallowed hard as I slowly nodded my consent. 'I will.' *Have you just told him a bare faced lie?*

I gave Greg a strained smile and a quick kiss on the cheek, stilling him from putting his coat on, hoping he would get the message I needed to be alone. With reluctance he said goodbye, watching me from the window as I almost ran down the street.

The cold air stung my cheeks a little as I hurried along. I felt I needed to gain some distance from their house before I could pluck

126

up the courage to phone Mum. Because of course I had to phone her. There's nothing else I can do with this utter bombshell. I needed to hear her reaction to know if this was true, and it couldn't wait till we saw each other face to face. I had too many questions burning away inside of me, leaving a hot feeling shooting down from my head to my stomach.

Does a mother's instinct kick-in? Does a ringing bell dong loudly in her head? Do you know immediately you need to stop whatever you're doing to answer your daughter? Do you have any idea that your locked up secrets are about to be ripped open?

The phone had barely even rang once when I heard my mother's voice. 'Lily?'

For a moment I was floored, totally unprepared for how to broach this. This mother I'd known all my life ...had somehow become someone new with a different dimension and depth. With hidden secrets I was never meant to know. A strange crippling shyness choked the words in my throat.

'Lily, are you there? What's wrong?' Her voice was worried now, sounding more like my mum and it gave me the courage to blurt out -

'I've just met Ted ... Greg's father ... He's told me everything, mum.'

There was a long excruciating pause. I held my breath, straining to hear her reaction.

Her voice, went it did come, was barely audible. 'Everything?'

'About you and him, yes.' I heard her intake of breath but ploughed on. 'But not why Dad wasn't with us when we stayed here. He, Ted, said you should be the one to tell me. Mum, I'm so confused! What's going on here? I feel like I don't know you-'

'I'm coming over on the next flight I can get.' Hannah broke in, a new steely determination in her voice. 'I'll call you when I arrive.'

'What?! No, Mum you don't need to-'

'I do. We can't talk about this over the phone .. and its time I faced up to this, told you the truth.... faced Dingle again. I'll text you with my flight details, darling. And please, don't worry. It's all okay.'

127

And with that she said goodbye and hung up. Leaving me suspended. Once more. Every aspect of my life seemed, right then, to be suspended. I wanted to take charge, run my own show, but too many factors and people seemed determined to prevent me. First Natalie, then David, Greg, Ted, and now Mum.

The urge to scream out loud took me by surprise, shocking me to the core. I fought it down but found myself breaking into a run, not caring which direction I took; as long as it rid me of this frustration and confusion weighing down my limbs.

I slowed down as I came to the bustling hustle of Main Street, the sweat trickling down my back leaving my skin feeling uncomfortable beneath my sweater. I pushed on up the hill and found myself slowing down to a stop outside "Cafe Peak". It was only around four pm but the lights were off, the closed sign firmly in place. Was it only a few hours ago I had been cosied up inside within its warmth and its owner, enjoying an intimacy I'd not felt in a very long time, if ever?

Now the cafe felt cold, repelling rather than inviting. I turned quickly away, my mind once more playing a questioning game of whether I should call David, or wait for him to make contact. *Oh this indecisiveness, I can't bear it! I'm going crazy here..*

With this thought, I pulled out my phone and, before I could talk myself out of it, I clicked on David's name, fired out a text "Thinking of you lots. Here if you need me xx", and swiftly pressed "send".

The text went zinging down the line focused on reaching its recipient.

David was sitting in his mum's lounge, trying and failing to tune out his mum and sister's heated conversation as he attempted to bond with his niece, who seemed set on playing a complicated game of snakes and ladders, where the rules kept changing. His phone vibrated against his leg. David yanked it out, saw the name and immediately opened it. A delighted smile brightened his face for a moment.

128

Then Lottie started pulling on his arm, bored already with the wait. With reluctance he shoved the phone back in his pocket without replying. As he refocused on his niece, a delighted, gleeful smile spread across her face in having got her own way.

David stilled, frozen, his breath intaking sharply. That smile, he knew that smile anywhere. And it wasn't her mum's or her grandma's familiar smile, but someone whose smile should not be on his niece's face....

Once more I found myself watching dawn break through the parting of the sunbeam curtains, the gentle sound of the rain surprisingly soothing against the window pane as I lay beneath my bedspread. I had slept badly, strange dis-jolted dreams of trying to reach some vague destination only to be frustratingly stopped at every turn, hindered by people trying to pull me back. My body had finally dragged me to wakefulness, and now I couldn't fall back to sleep.

A while later I caught up with Ciara downstairs as she bustled about in her usual cheery manner. In that moment I envied her; her confidence in who she was and what she was doing in her little corner of the world, even if I caught an occasional whiff of sadness about her.

'Ciara.' I called out to her.

'With you in a minute, lovely!'

I grabbed some cereal, then took my usual seat. I was one of only three guests now – the summer season was over and with it the best of the trade. Ireland was beautiful, but not renowned for its weather at the best of times, let alone as we moved into September.

Ciara came over with a pot of english breakfast tea without asking first; which comforted me somehow.

'Like one of my special Irish's?'

I shook my head with a smile. 'If I eat anymore of those I wont be able to fit into my last comfy pair of jeans!'

'You look better for it if you ask me, with a bit of flesh on your bones and cheeks.'

'I don't think my bank balance can afford to keep me on this new 'diet'... Don't worry, I'm fine with just some cereal. But I wanted to ask, my mum is arriving later today -'

'Ah well that's lovely! What's her name?' Ciara smiled.

'Hannah. I know this is *really* short notice but do you have a spare room you can put her into for just a couple of nights before we both head back home?'

'Of course, no problem, I have just the room for her. But well now, are you going to be leaving us?'

Her disappointed words cut straight to me. I fought back an irrational urge to cry. 'I'm afraid so ... though given half a chance I would stay here.' I admitted, hesitating for just a moment before continuing, 'I feel like this is home, Ciara.'

She nodded as she pondered this. 'I think that you do. I think that you do belong here. You fit well. And does... David know?' Her eyes searched mine as she asked the pointed question.

'Sort of.' I answered vaguely. *Has he realised? And if so, does it matter to him?*

'Maybe it would be good to have a chat then, with him?' Ciara encouraged. 'If that's the man you feel strongly about?' She continued to probe.

'Yes ...' I nodded, taking refuge in my tea, with the feeling that Ciara had been trying to ask me much more than she'd verbally said. I raised my head to ask her just that, but she had already vanished from the room.

So instead I sit mulling. Bottom line? I would love nothing more than to do just that; sit and talk with him. But it was feeling more and more like I 'd been given all the time I would have with him ... and I couldn't bury my head in the sand any longer.

I sat now half-heartedly repacking my suitcase, as my mind continued to play things over.

130

I was so aware I needed to gain some courage to say goodbye, face to face, to Greg ... and to David. To say goodbye over the phone or text was just inexcusable, cowardly even. For my own sake, I needed to see David and know he wanted me to go...

So when my phone buzzed from where it lay abandoned on the bed, I almost disbelieved it when it told me I had received a text from David.

I found I was almost hesitant in opening it, even though I had been desperate to hear from him. I found myself tensing up as I pressed 'open'.

"Sorry for not replying b4 all been a bit crazy here. Can you come over to the café?"

My fingers flew over the phone "On my way xx"

After running a brush through my hair and reapplying lip gloss, I rushed out of the door.

A feeling of optimism coursed through me as I headed down into the main part of town.

A lifting away of holding my breath, of stifling inaction. At last, thank you God! Whatever happened between us in the next few hours, I just felt mentally better for the chance to fight for him. For us...

I came up to the café, took a breath, unconsciously smoothing down my hair, then pushed open the door.

There were a few customers enjoying a leisurely coffee and catch up, some with smiles on their faces, others with a deep frown of concern in their eyes as they shared their woes. My eyes darted to the counter, expecting to see David in his usual spot. But only Dora stood there, mixing a cappuccino.

A little confused, I scanned the room to see if he was chatting to someone, or coming in from the back storeroom.

But no, he wasn't there. I was just taking out my phone to call him, when I heard someone call my name. A woman's voice.

131

I felt a strange prickling on my skin, a rushing in my blood. Slowly I lifted my head and looked straight across at her.

Natalie sat there, composed, alone, a small smile hovering on her lips.

I found my feet walking towards her, a thousand questions already jostling for top position.

I sat down opposite her, taking her properly in. It was the woman from my photo.. and yet it wasn't. She was far more stunning in the flesh, those same blue eyes as David's now searching my face, as if looking for immediate answers. And still far more composed and calm then I had been prepared for; almost uncomfortably so.

'Hello Lily. How are you?'

'Umm fine, thank you. Is … is David here?' I cast another quick look around the café, still vainly hoping, still confused by this sudden change of events.

'He'll be here soon. I'm sorry.' Natalie's eyes held a note of apology, but a steely determination none the less. 'I asked him to invite you here so we could chat. In private. Is that okay?"

'Yes, I guess so.' I answered though felt like there wasn't much choice in the matter. 'I'm a little taken aback. But I think I might have as many questions as I do answers for you.'

She nodded. 'Would you like a coffee or tea, maybe something else?'

I shook my head. 'No, I'm fine at the moment, thanks.'

I waited to see what she would say. In truth, I was flummoxed. How do we broach this, even begin to rationalise and explain how I came to be in her life, to be a spoke in the wheel that has caused this uncovering of her and her child, when perhaps she'd been content to remain where she was? Without sparing her or her feelings, we had gone into the shadows and drawn her out, without let-up or mercy. As that thought struck me, I felt guilt course through me. No doubt she must be very resentful of me.

But she'd called out to me! I know that, I know that. I can't forget it, no matter what mask she was presenting to me today. There was a reason for all of this. There had to be... surely.

132

I broke the silence first. I couldn't bear it any longer. 'I know you must be confused as to why I'm so personally involved with you and your family. I know we're technically strangers-'

'Actually we're not.'

That stopped me sharply in my tracks. I stared at her. 'What do you mean?'

Her head cocked to one side, as she absently stirred her almost cold untouched coffee. 'Do you not remember me, Lily?' At my continued mystified stare, Natalie continued, 'As children? We played together one summer when you were staying here.'

My mind swept back, to that unsettling dream of me standing on the beach, a girl with two other children calling out to me, though her features had been blurred. It must have been Natalie! With what I'd just discovered about my mum, it was all beginning to make sense.

'David had reached that age of not wanting to be around his little sister, so I was glad to have you to play with. For some reason I've never forgotten you, or that summer. Can you remember any of it? Remember me?'

'A little now.' I admitted. I leaned forward. 'I remember a beach, a girl who must be you. But that's years ago ...why appear to me now?'

There was a significant withdrawal in her body language on hearing my words. She looked away. 'David told me you started the search with him for me. That I "appeared" to you... '

The way she said it, condescending and cool, told me all I needed to know. Without doubt she saw me as some mad stalker. And I couldn't just leave it like that, damn it! I leaned further forward, wanting her to trust me, open up to me. Help us both to understand this.

'Natalie, I know, trust me I know, how odd this all sounds. Please rest assured that I'm not some crazy lunatic out to stir up trouble, or stalk you for the rest of your life.'

She gave a reluctant half smile at that, though her eyes remained cool. 'I'm glad to hear it.'

'I don't understand this any more than you. It makes no rational sense, end of. *But* you appeared to me with such impact that I found myself putting my whole life on hold. I felt a pull so strong, like you needed me to help find you.'

Natalie gave a nonchalant shrug. 'I'm not sure why that would be the case. I'm fine, just fine.'

Really?

Something in her manner, of trying to be too offhand, somehow didn't ring true. When I would naturally back away and apologise for interfering, I found myself instead staring rather hard at her until her gaze faltered and she turned her face away. A tremor flickered in her cheek. Her body was taut.

'I don't think that you are, Natalie.' I softly replied.

She closed her eyes for a moment, fiddled with her coffee again. I waited patiently until she had no choice but to look up. And hoped there would be some breaking down in her, just as there had been in David.

But as she locked her eyes with mine I saw that whatever emotion, whatever chink in her steel armour I had slightly got under, was now firmly put back under control. I had lost her again. Her voice, and her manner, edged towards brutal coldness.

'I know you may mean well. I know you and my brother have grown close through this. But I don't need you. At all.' Her eyes bore hard into mine. I shrunk back a little against the force, swallowing hard. 'I only came back to let mam and David know I'm okay and let them meet Lottie. To have kept them apart till now … well it's just one more guilty sin I've learnt to carry.'

Even if I had wanted to inject, which I didn't, she left me with no room to do so as she stormed on as if she was determined to take command. 'I suppose I should let you know that I'm leaving again, probably to somewhere new.'

For a moment I froze, poleaxed. I even hoped I'd heard her wrong. But one look into her eyes and I knew I hadn't misunderstood. That she had the audacity to tell me this after everything! My anger rose, searing a hot flame up through my body.

'You can't leave – not now! It would devastate your mum, David-'

'I have no choice. Nothing has changed on that. I can't … breathe here. You must keep this to yourself. I want you to promise me, Lily. You owe me that.'

'No, don't ask me that.' My voice was pitched with new despair. 'What could be so bad about living back here with Lottie? Starting again?'

Something I said hit a raw spot, her coldness dimming just for a moment. She gave a soft tiny moan, shaking her head. 'You don't understand. How can you? Lottie ...'

'What? What about Lottie? Tell me!'

'He's here.'

'Here? Who's here?!'

Her eyes clashed with mine, sparking anger. 'Don't be stupid as well as blind! He lives here, Lily, he lives here. Don't you get it?!'

'What?' I asked again stupidly, though what she was trying to tell me was slowly penetrating my dulled brain.

'He can't ever be a proper dad to her. Ever.'

The words were delivered with a finality I could not ignore. And with a hidden despair I could not turn away from.

Chapter Eighteen

His voice cut through our suspended silence.

'Lottie's Dad lives here?'

We both swung our heads up, startled, to see David standing there looming over us. I saw an unmistakeable flinch in Natalie's cheek as she stared up at him, challenging him almost. I pulled David down to the chair beside me. He held her gaze with sheer grit and determination to stop her evading his question.

Yet, somehow, she did exactly that, an expert it seemed in avoiding the truth and having uncomfortable conversations.

'Yes ... but that's all I can tell you. You weren't suppose to know even that.' She added in a dark mutter.

'No, Nat! That's not enough, for pity's sake! You need to tell me who he is so we can properly sort this all out. Is he paying you child maintenance for a start? Does Lottie have proper visiting access set up? What-'

She gave an exasperated wave of her hand. 'It's all fine, don't worry. Her Dad and I have a good arrangement... we're well provided for.'

David raised his eyebrows, remembering the state of the flat's door, and the rest of the buildings' condition.

'Do I know him, Nat?'

The question came without warning. Something in his voice put me on high alert, and Natalie also ... like he had already suspected, but wanted her to disprove him. My mind raced to try and keep up with him. *Who was he thinking of? Am I thinking the same as him, unconsciously?*

She merely stared stubbornly back at him, giving him no answer, nothing at all.

David closed his eyes for a moment, then tried a different tactic. 'And does he know that you're both here now?'

Natalie paused, looking from one to the other, reminding me of a deer caught in the headlights of an oncoming car. 'No, not yet ...'

David and I shared an aghast look. I broke in. 'Why not? Isn't that going to cause a problem when he sees you both, especially if you're with us?'

She closed her eyes for a moment, pulling her hair back from her face, showing agitation for the first time. 'I know, I know! I'm going to call him in a minute. In fact,' she went to rise from the table, her body stiff and hard. 'I'm going now. I'll call you later.'

And with that she was gone, leaving us staring at her recent vacated place.

I turned to look at David, itching to grill him on what he thought, who he suspected Lottie's father was. He sat frozen, deep worry lines etched across his face. I yearned to reach out and pull him close to me. Hold him tight, soothe away the worry. My hand even reached up. But the overwhelming absence of him from the last two days, so soon after our growing intimacy, was leaving me with a compounding shyness I couldn't just shake off.

He turned to look at me. For a moment, the distraction in his face remained. Then I must have come into his full focus, I could see it in his eyes, his warmer gaze. He smiled and I felt a responding smile spread across mine, unabashed joy exploding within me.

'Hi.' He said.

'Hi.' I replied, holding his gaze as steadily as I could.

Our hands reached out, entwined around the other.

'Will you come and walk with me? I could do with some fresh air after this latest "revelation" ...unless you need to be somewhere else.' He added as he saw me give my watch the tiniest of glances.

I bit my lip, torn. 'I have to meet my mum soon.'

Seeing his surprised look, I explained. 'She's coming to Dingle today. It's all been going on for me too.' I grimaced, 'But I really want to spend time with you. Maybe we could take a short one? I might have to head off though when she calls to say she's arrived.'

'Sure, sure, of course. If its only a few minutes, then that's what I will take. Come on.'

With my hand tightly grasped in his, we made our way out.

'The last couple of days have been bonkers.' David shook his head as he gazed out across the water. We were sitting straddling the stone wall at the end of the harbour, our hands still clasped together.

For a while it'd been enough to just simply be, watch the soothing motion of the boats sailing in and out of the harbour, bobbing gently on the water. Now, David began to open up.

'Completely exhausting; mentally and emotionally ... especially breaking the news about Dad. She just broke down in tears.'

'I can imagine.' And I could. *But my goodness its hard to tally up this picture with the cold girl I have just talked with.* I paused, wanting to push down any resenting feelings trying to rear their ugly head. I cocked my head a little, forehead creasing. 'Even though we'd been searching for her, it was still a shock to see Natalie standing there, wasn't it?'

'Just a little...! And Nat has this ability to make you think she'd only left last week and was always planning to come back, as if it's her way of justifying her actions. But I can't, and wont, just let her off that easily. She's hurt so many people and she needs to understand that.' He turned to me, frowning hard. 'And not to tell us about Lottie – that's what hurt mam and me the most.'

'Of course it did. Absolutely! Everything you're feeling now you're 110% entitled to feel!' I urged strongly, a passionate note to my voice. 'None of you can just sweep this under the carpet, pretend the last five years haven't happened. It's not good or healthy to do that.'

David nodded, his eyes clouded. 'I know.' He sighed. 'I know you're right. But as you have now experienced for yourself, Nat can be one very stubborn, evasive woman. Especially when it comes to telling us whose Lottie's father is...'

I trod carefully. 'Do you have any clue who it might be? It's a close knit community here...'

A nerve flinched in his cheek. 'I have a feeling... but I'm hoping I'm wrong. Could be a coincidence.' His eyes flickered back to mine. 'I need to talk to Sean.'

As he said Sean's name, my mind flashed back to the scene in the pub with his wife Amy. Something still troubled me there, a clue given that my frustrated brain hadn't yet grasped on to. Then there was the way David just said his name.

I gave a little concerned nod. 'Okay... maybe he can help.'

'Let's wait and see, shall we?'

I gazed at David, then at a small chartered fishing boat as it smoothly docked into the harbour, my mind all the while whirling at a furious pace. *I need to warn him Natalie might leave again, I can't have that on my conscience... And that I'm leaving too..*

I was bracing myself to say this when David's hand suddenly cupped my cheek, his touch gently coaxing my face round to his. Then his lips were on mine and I instantly responded, drawing him as close to me as I could as we kissed.

When we pulled apart, David was smiling as he brushed my hair back from my forehead.

'I've been wanting to do that since we last kissed.' He admitted, gently tugging at my curls to bring my face closer to his again.

In response, I kissed him again, then in reluctance pulled back from his embrace. As I did, David bore a sudden guilty look. 'Sorry. I've been so caught up in my family dramas I've not asked you why your mam is coming here.'

I gave a soft groan. 'You're not the only one who has family members harbouring secrets right here in Dingle.'

With that, I relayed him the full story, including what Natalie had just told me. David looked as suitably shocked by this as I had felt.

I was just coming to the end when my phone started ringing loudly, intrusively. As I saw my mum's name flashing on the phone, my heart sank a little. *No... why this moment? I just wanted ten more minutes with David. I'm not even emotionally prepared to see her..*

I tried hard not to show any of this inner conflict as I answered. 'Hi mum, have you landed?'

139

'Yes darling, I've landed. I just need to catch the bus and should be with you within half an hour. Where shall I meet you?'

I wanted to be selfish, just this once, and let her take the bus. Allow me just a few more precious minutes with David.

But it seemed a daughter's guilt would always be the stronger pull. I couldn't do it. I tried to conceal my sigh as I replied. 'No, don't be silly. Stay there, I'll drive over and pick you up. I'll see you in the entrance area shortly.'

We hung up. I closed my eyes for a moment. I felt David's hand stroke my hand. As I opened them, I saw concern and kindness in his as he searched my face.

'Do you want me to come with you, support you?'

Uncharacteristic tears sprung into my eyes. 'I would love you to .. but I think Mum and I need to do this alone. Can I call you after?'

'Of course you can. You don't even need to ask that.' His hand continued to stroke mine soothingly.

I nodded, managed to blurt out, 'We need to talk too.'

His hand stilled on mine. A look of alarm crossed his face. 'We do?'

I could not look at him, my emotions had gone crazy. I pulled him into a hug, my arms around his neck. I felt his slowly go around me, a thousand unsaid words between us. I brought my mouth to his ear. Whispered then, 'I'll be going home with mum tomorrow. I have to go... because my reason for coming here is no more.'

I was pulled sharply back so I had to look at him. '*What*?! No, hold on, you can't, Lil, you can't just go off and leave like that!' His voice was demanding, angry even but I could hear the underlying emotions governing it. He was staring at me, shaking his head forcefully. In one way I rejoiced at seeing this reaction, in another wondering if was just because he had come to rely on me to be a steady companion throughout all this - a very different emotion to wanting to be with someone as your lifetime partner, lover, friend.

I forced myself to gently disentangle myself from him, swinging my leg over to stand up.

'Lil, wait-'

140

I stopped him with a kiss that sent a tremor through us both. ' I'll call you later, I promise.'

Before he could stop me, I turned and walked rapidly back up the harbour side, trying in vain to hold back the tears.

It isn't goodbye yet. Not yet..

Kerry airport was surprisingly busy today for its size and capacity. I strained to see over the numerous mix of blonde, brunette and black heads, mingled in with the odd silver and white one. A mild wave of panic hit me that somehow I had missed mum, that she had gone on ahead anyway.

But just as I was starting to pull out my phone, I heard my mum's distinct english voice calling my name. I looked up and saw her walking towards me.

I smiled and waved, but my smile was heavy, hesitant, as if it didn't quite know how to greet Mum in a normal way. I was feeling odd, out of sorts. To confuse me even more, Mum pulled me into a tight, almost awkward hug as soon as she was close to me, the bags still gripped in her hand. I hugged her back, taken aback. *Mum normally just kisses me quickly on the cheek, not embrace me like this.. like she doesn't want to let go.*

I reached down and grabbed her small overnight suitcase, needing a distraction and the steadiness it brought. 'Ready to go?'

Mum let out a breath then slowly nodded. 'I'm ready.' She looked pale beneath her brave smile. *This is painful for her too, I can see that now.*

We chatted inanimately as I drove us back the now familiar route to Dingle. I told her about the people I'd met here, but held back from saying too much about David ... there was more pressing things on Mum's mind then to give me advice on my churned up feelings for him. *Maybe later...*

I couldn't fail to notice the physical change wash over mum as we drew nearer. She seemed to grow fidgety, straining to look ahead, her hands restless in her lap. I was about to ask her if she was alright when she suddenly pointed towards the brown sign for 'Inch beach'.

'Can we go for a walk there? I used to love walking on Inch beach.'

I could only stare incredibly at her for a moment, before clearing my throat and quietly say, 'Me too.'

The air felt heavy today as we walked slowly along the beach. It felt different to touch this familiar sand with mum beside me. I guess I'd come to see this as my own sanctuary, my private refuge. Now I had to accept a different feel, a different meaning, a place that clearly held memories and history for mum. And I really didn't know how I felt about that, or even how to react.

We continued along, the silence stretching out as far as the distant horizon. A few times I almost opened my mouth to say something, then squeezed my lips shut agin. At last, thank goodness, she broke the silence.

'I want you to understand that this changes nothing about how you should remember your Dad. In every other way he is still the man you knew growing up, the man who was with us till quite recently.' She stopped, turned to me, making me nearly stumble in my haste to stop too. Her eyes forced mine to hold hers. 'You understand, darling, what I'm saying?'

I stared at her, found myself nodding when really what I wanted to do was scream, *No I don't understand!*

Mum seemed satisfied and resumed her walk, staring straight ahead. Her voice was caught by the wind so I stepped closer, straining to catch every word.

'Your Dad could be such a private man, it was hard to know what he was thinking, feeling. When we first met he was more open, talked to me about what was going on in his head. But as the years went on, somehow instead of trusting in me more, he withdraw further. It killed me at the time. Eventually, you were born after many years of trying and I think then because I had someone else to love and care for, it took away some of the hurt he'd caused me. We had a few money problems which didn't help. The pressure can be immense as the sole breadwinner and provider. But I never thought that it would cause him to simply walk away from us...'

I stopped dead, forcing mum to follow suit. 'He left us?' I gasped, my face paling.

She stared at me 'He left me.' She corrected. 'He never intentionally left you.'

'But I... I don't ... why?!'

Hannah sighed, rubbed her forehead unconsciously. 'I guess he wanted to retreat from the world for a while. Run away. There was always something not quite right, something from his past he could never tell me. But he left us in a mess, a complete mess. If it hadn't been for you ... Anyway, I kept going, what else could I do? I just told you Dad was working away and you seemed happy to accept that.' She turned and stared without seeing across the expanse of the water.

My memory was stirring, strange images coming back, a vaguest sense of a time without Dad.

'It was nearly six months later when I started to get these phone calls.'

'What kind of phone calls?'

'Ones where you go to pick up and the caller hangs up before saying anything.' Mum turned to me. 'It was your Dad, I knew it was. So I got hold of the number he was calling from, called it. It was a guest house here in Dingle. Suddenly I was filled with anger. How dare he leave us with little money while he enjoyed freedom and pleasure in Dingle?' The long ago anger sparked in her eyes even now. I tried not to show my shock at seeing its devastating depths. But I too felt a slow growing anger towards my Dad; a useless anger against a man who was no longer alive to take the brunt of it.

'Why Dingle?'

She gave a little shrug. 'I don't know. I don't think your Dad knew why either. Perhaps it was the first place he got to. Anyway I took you with me to Dingle to try and find him, confront him. But of

143

course, life doesn't always play out in the way you want it too ... instead it pushes you into someone else's life with no thought to the consequences.'

She stopped again, bit her lip, turned away. But I moved round till she had no choice but to look me in the eye.

'You mean Ted ... you met Ted?'

'Yes.' She said, simply.

I took a deep shuddering breath to calm myself enough to say, 'And you fell in love.'

'Yes ... when I wasn't looking or searching for it.'

'And what about Dad when all this was happening? Did you give up on finding him?!' My misplaced anger was burning inside of me, desperate to find a deserving villain in the story.

'No! I never gave up! But what do you do when a man doesn't want to be found, tell me that?!'

I couldn't push it down anymore. The anger burst out of me. 'I don't know! I don't know about any of this! There's this whole part of my life you're suddenly sharing with me and its scaring me rigid! Its like I must have blanked out this whole part even though everyone is telling me I was here, that I made friends with Greg, Natalie, David. But I barely remember any of it, I don't Mum!'

She pulled me into a hug, stroking my head, calming me down. 'Its okay, its alright.' She soothed, 'I know this is all of a shock to you. We should have told you. But we thought it was best to forget about it, brush it away. It was the wrong thing to do, I can see that now.'

I raised my head to stare at her, still trying desperately to figure it all out. 'I know Dad came home, he must have done because he was there throughout my teens and twenties.'

'Eventually he did, but not while we were here. A few weeks after we got back to England, he arrived, still telling me nothing but that he was sorry and wouldn't do it again. There was no big emotional confrontation for us here in Dingle, no release for me. In the end I had to leave here before ... I couldn't .'

144

Suddenly she grasped my arms, a desperation in her voice. 'How is he? How's Ted?'

I wanted to lie to protect us both, tell her that he wished her well but was happy in his marriage. In fact, I opened my mouth to say exactly that. But I made the mistake of looking into her eyes, her eyes which showed the depths of feeling still harboured after all these years. Eyes that held a grief and despair I'd never before seen, or wanted to see.

The words tumbled out. 'He's never forgotten you, Mum. He carries the same look in his eyes as you do now.'

To my dismay, a tear fell down her cheek. 'Saying goodbye to him … it was horrendous. We couldn't even say goodbye properly because you and Greg suddenly appeared.'

I stepped back, my hand flying to my mouth. This time a memory came back so vividly it felt like I was standing right there in it. I saw myself walking up from this beach, a boy beside me. I remember seeing my mum standing with a man crying and he holding onto her tight. Of me calling out her name and the despair in her eyes as she turned blindly to me. Of me then running away until I stumbled into my dark haired girl friend. The boy Greg, the girl Natalie...

Mum was saying something, something important, ultimately dangerous. It forced me to push the memory away, to be here in the present. I gave myself a shake, refocused on mum.

'What did you just say?'

She gave an almost impatient sigh. 'I said I need to see him. I have to see him. Now.'

Hannah turned and began running over the sand. I stumbled as I chased after her. 'No wait! Mum, please! That's not a good idea.'

'Until you've found real love you can't possibly understand this, Lil! Please, just take me to him.'

'You're wrong! I do know now what real love is, Mum. But this can't possibly be the right way to go about it!'

She stopped, spun round. Every word was delivered with determination, and passion. 'It is exactly the right way. Now will you please take me or do I need to find a different way of getting there?'

Chapter Nineteen

I understood her conviction, yet I couldn't rejoice in it. I felt she was about to open up old wounds, with no hope of satisfying healing. After all, nothing had changed for Ted in his own personal situation. He was still married, to my friend's mum.

We pulled up near to their home. I cut the engine, stared straight ahead for a moment, before turning to look at mum. A knot of tension gripped my stomach painfully.

She was gazing over to the bungalow, lost to me already.

'It's just as I remember it, exactly the same.' She murmured

'Yes ... with the same wife and son, a son who is a friend of mine.' I emphasised as strongly as I dared.

One swift look at her face and I knew my attempt at reasoning was falling on death ears.

Mum gave a soft gasp. I swung my head to follow her direction. Ted had come out of the door, was now waiting silently, patiently, for her. As if he'd known this moment he had been dreaming of … was here.

Is it possible to have a sixth sense like that? It's true that I've felt a strong sense of something before. Or perhaps 'a feeling' would be a better way to describe it, particularly when I knew, *just knew,* I wouldn't see someone close to me again ... that this would be the last time I would watch them walk off.

I'd felt that with Dad two years again. We had said our normal goodbye with a quick hug as I left them after a meal one evening. I remember this urge to want to uncharacteristically hold on tight to him, not let go, then to turn back one more time to see his smile and wave as I pulled out of the driveway. The very next morning he was gone from me because of a sudden heart attack in the night. Had it been God telling me to not let this moment go by unnoticed?

But what would Dad make of this now? Was he watching in disbelief, as I was, in seeing my mum, *my mum* who had somehow transformed into this different unknown person to the one I 'd always known, get out of my car and take one, two, then faster steps towards the man she'd carried in her heart for so long?

I heard a sob and it took me a moment to comprehend it had come from within the depths of me. I felt strange, disorientated, as if I wasn't really here in this car watching this woman and man suddenly cling to each other.

I turned on the engine, wanting, *needing* to get away.

Mum never even turned around as I screeched off.

I don't remember parking the car, but now found myself outside "Cafe Peak". It was dusk and the light was slowly ebbing away. I looked in. A couple of customers were still drawing out their almost cold coffees. I could see David and Dora clearing away, laughing about something. I found myself smiling as I watched them.

Something made me resist walking straight in. Instead I pulled out my phone. Perhaps a small part of me wanted to see how he'd react in seeing my name appear on his phone. Or maybe I just wanted to look at him, savour him in his natural environment, at ease with himself. Whatever drove me, I wasn't disappointed. I saw him pull out his phone from where it rang in his pocket, smile broadly and quickly answer it. His voice felt warm and reassuring as I turned to lean against the wall, hugging myself, smiling with an immense feeling of relief.

'Hey, been thinking of you since you left. Are you okay? Has your mam got here safely?'

'Hey back... I'm okay. Kind of. Lots to take in, and tell you about. Can we meet up later?'

'Of course, of course. Ah, only thing is I've promised to take Nat to the pub in about an hour. I think its time she saw Sean and Amy. Come and join us, sure we could slip away after a while.' I was about to voice my instant concern about his planned surprise for his friends, but got distracted when David added, 'I really want to see you badly.'

147

'Me too …' *So much.*

'So I'll see you there about seven then?'

I found myself agreeing and calling off. I could not help turning around one last time to gaze at him as he slipped his phone away, resume his clearing up. There was a joy to his actions, as if he was coming to a place of peace, at last.

My heart contracted with a profound fear for him. The weight of knowledge and my own suspicions were laying heavily at my feet. I felt he shared them too, but still, I may be wrong on that. But no matter what, all I could do was protect him, and try to soften the blows of what was still to come.

Barely twenty minutes later, I found myself doing something I didn't think I would ever do again …venturing in to see PC Daryl. Especially when he was closing up the station for the evening, his hand poised ready to turn the key.

He paused as he spotted me smiling hopefully at him, and I swear he muttered, 'Oh just what I need.' as he reluctantly opened the door to me.

'I was about to close.' Came his first words, though he did allow me to take a couple of steps into his hallowed room.

'I know, I wont keep you long, I promise.' I hastily said, feeling like a naughty schoolgirl coming to see the headmaster. 'I wanted to ask if you had any information on a different person this time.'

PC Daryl raised his eyebrows in surprise. 'Another person? Are you opening up your own missing persons bureau or something?'

His comment had a surprising effect on me and I found myself giving a short delighted laugh. This seemed to create a positive reaction in him, for a faint smile hovered on his lips and now he asked me in a more friendly voice, 'What makes you think I might be any more help this time?'

'I don't ... but I'm just hoping.' I admitted. 'Its my dad, Anthony Crossways. He lived here quite some time back, in the nineties. 1992 to be precise. I just wondered if he had had any contact with you here...'

It sounded a little mad, my theory, when said out loud. I had come here on a hunch, a pure hunch. Now I was feeling a little stupid and was beginning to back away. 'Sorry, I know you wont have anything on him-'

'Stay put.' He sighed heavily, 'I'll go and check our old filing cabinets at the back.'

Obediently I sat down on a nearby chair and waited for what felt like a very long time, absently studying the posters adorning the walls reminding me to report any suspicious behaviour ... *should I report myself?!*

Eventually PC Daryl came back in ... and was carrying a thin brown file. I stared in shock at it.

He sat down beside me, and paused for a moment, meeting my eyes for the first time. For some reason that made me feel very nervous.

'I do have some information on your father. It seemed he was arrested on one occasion-

'Arrested?! My Dad?!'

'Yes, for causing a disturbance at one of our local drinking establishments.' He opened the file, scanning the notes quickly. 'Nothing major, appeared to be some disagreement over money your father owed to a local bed and breakfast. Your father took offence, they got into a fight, he spent the night here with the local constable. No formal charges as the debt appeared to be paid by a friend ... no name given. Then your father left Dingle soon after. And that's all that's in here.'

I found myself staring at him, completely poleaxed. It was only when he cleared his throat and rather pointedly looked at his watch that I was able to shake myself enough to stand up, though everything in me itched to reach out and grab the file, so I could convince myself it was authentic.

'Sorry, sorry, I'll let you close up. Um ... thank you, thanks.'

'No problem. Hope it helps.'

I found myself outside once again, faintly aware of the lights going out behind me and the door being determinedly locked.

Okay, so what do I do with this information?!

Shaking my head I began to wander aimlessly up the path in the vague direction of 'Smugglers'.

As I did, I became aware of a older looking lady, hair as white as freshly laid snow, her clothes practical rather than glamourous, who stood across the road from me. She seemed to be watching me, her body poised and stiff. Noticing me noticing her, she hesitated for the briefest moment, then started to cross the road towards me. I frowned, trying to recognise her in the gloomy growing dusk. She came up real close and I noticed her eyes were dark, fathomless, unreadable. She was a little taller then me. She hesitated again for the briefest moment then plunged in. Her voice was croaky and strongly accented with the local dialect.

'Hello now. Sorry to bother you and all... do you recognise me?'

I shook my head in apology, trying hard to place her when she so definitely thought she knew me. 'Sorry, I don't think I do...'

'I'm Eliana ... Greg's mam.'

'Oh!' I couldn't keep the exclamation out of my voice. I recovered a little and attempted to smile. 'It's good to meet you. I know your son, he's been great, and of course your husband...'

I trailed off, flushing, realising that was not a good conversation for us to be having. At all. An awful thought captured my brain. *Oh no, have my mum and Ted said something to her?! Were they together at her house now? Declared they were running off together-*

She cut into my frantic, panicked thoughts. 'I know, and probably its best we don't talk about Greg or my husband ...under the circumstances. I'm sure you understand, no?'

Her eyes were surprisingly steely and I found myself nodding fast. 'Okay.' I felt on the wrong foot here, and had no idea how to proceed. *What does she want from me? Does she want me to stay away from Greg? Or talk to my mum..*

Eliana gave a short sigh. 'Listen, I'm sure you mean well being here. I don't hold anything against you. You were just a wee girl caught up in the middle of family stuff. ' She squared her shoulders, I didn't take my eyes off her for a second. 'But I thought you should know that before your mam and you came here, we tried to help your pa, Ted and me. He got into a bit of trouble, financially, and we felt sorry for him, I guess. He seemed .. troubled. We lent him a little money, not much. Not that he was able to pay it back.' Seeing my aghast look, she waved her hand as if to dismiss it. Perhaps she had learnt to wave aside lots of troubles, conflicts, emotions over the years. All at once, an overwhelming feeling of pity for her cut through me. That and guilt, so so much guilt that it was my family causing this renewed upset for her now, more pain for her to try and wave aside.

'I'm sorry my family seem to have caused you trouble.' I felt compelled to say, however inconsequential those words were; meaningless even.

She smiled a little ironically at that. 'Yes, that's the truth, for sure. If I'd known what was coming...' Eliana turned her head away and I stood there a little unsure, flummoxed. I was opening my mouth to say something, anything, to stop this excruciating conversation, when her voice cut through. 'He knew Iona better, your pa. Maybe you should talk to her. I just thought you had the right to know. I know what's it like to be kept in the dark.'

Her words were uttered from a tormented place, but her body and manner were now determined to shut me out.

Without another word, Eliana pivoted away from me, disappearing up the street.

Leaving me standing there, pulled in every which way.

Chapter Twenty

As soon as I stepped through its doors and saw Greg, a strangling kind of reticence took ahold of me. I mean, what was I meant to say?! *Heard the story about your Dad and my mum being a little more than just friends? Or how about how the one about both your parents knowing my Dad and helping him out of a 'bit of bother'? And the best bit? We might get to be one big happy family, future step-brother!*

Mmm exactly...

But I was crap at maintaining a pretence, and couldn't lie to him either. So my best hope was to try to buy a little time before Mum and Ted decided what they were doing. For all I knew they might just be catching up. No-one else need know there was more at risk here... I certainly wasn't about to start telling everyone.

I gave myself a mental shake, before going up to where Greg stood in his usual spot. He looked up as he saw me, gave a smile …but it wasn't quite up to its normal wide stretch. I felt immediate panic rise up within me. Did he know already? Had his mum come in here first to tell him before seeking me out? *Or was something else afoot here?*

I gingerly perched myself on the stool and waited patiently for him to come over to me.

'Long time no see.' He offered as a hello.

I probed deep into his eyes. They were troubled, had lost their normal cheeky sparkle.

'Are you alright, Greg?'

He gave a little shrug, as if to brush off the comment as quickly as possible. 'Sure, sure, top of the world as normal.'

I reached out to touch his hand, concern spreading through me. 'Really? Are you really alright? Because it seems to me like you're troubled about something.'

The last of his forced smile slipped away. He looked down, then away before finally turning back to me. His fingers moved to hold mine.

'Something is wrong at home, something has altered everything between my parents. They are even more strained with one another, if that's possible. ' He gave a short humourless laugh, before sighing. 'I can't fathom what it is though and nobody, dammit, trusts me enough to tell me!' The words were burst out of him, borne out of frustration.

They could not fail to ignite a strong sense of guilt in my heart. I tried to form the right words in my mind, was about to try them out for real, when I felt a hand pressing into the small of my back. I looked up to see David standing there, silently watching the two of us. I was aware of the shadow of Natalie just behind him. David's eyes held a questioning look, then narrowed as they took in my hands still linked with Greg. I pulled my hand back, inwardly cursing.

Greg's features altered so rapidly I blinked in surprise. His voice was painfully bright.

'Good to see you, Davey. How are you doing on this fine evening? And whose this gorgeous girl with you?'

David gave a startled laugh. 'Greg, you must remember my sister, Natalie?!'

'We certainly all got up to enough trouble when we were young... ' Natalie stepped forward, smiling.

Greg looked astounded for a long moment, then his face broke into a huge grin. 'Nat, of course! What am I like? I *knew* that photo of you looked very familiar!' He leaned over the counter to give her a kiss on each cheek, enthused with excitement. 'So good to see my partner in crime again after all these years. How are you? What happened to all that short blond hair and scary make-up?'

Momentary pause, then, 'I'm good, it's good to be back. I decided to go back to my roots.'

Greg turned and gave David a narrowed, suspicious look. 'Why didn't you say it was her when Lily here first showed you the photo?'

153

I held my breath, wondering how David was going to get out of this one. I needn't have worried, David had no trouble smoothing over the deepest cracks this time.

'Wanted to surprise you all, of course. Worked, eh?'

Greg shook his head. 'It sure did. It sure did. Well, I think this calls for the first ones on the house in honour of our gang's reunion.'

'Excellent!' We all grinned in pleasure.

'I'll wait for these, you two go find a table.' Nat offered quickly. Too quickly. As if she was reluctant to leave the safety of the bar. I gazed over at her. She seemed nervous, jumpy. Which is not surprising, I told myself sternly. *Stop reading more into this then there is.*

We obeyed her, I for one glad to have David all to myself for a moment.

'Please don't read anything into Greg and I.' I urged, leaning close.

David looked away from staring at the pub door and turned to me. 'I'm trying not to, but when you said we needed to talk I couldn't help wondering if it was to tell me you and him...'

He let the sentence trail off and I hastened to reassure. 'Oh no, no! I promise you, at least on my part, I have no romantic feelings towards Greg. He's more like a … brother.' Was the only word I could grope for, though the ironic humour of that wasn't lost on me.

There was a moment of unconcealed relief on his face. Then David grinned, and I couldn't help grinning back. 'Good to hear that.' He mumbled before quickly kissing me.

'Glad to be of help.' I murmured back as we headed towards our favourite corner booth. As we sat down, my face sobered. 'But I think my family are about to cause Greg unfair misery... Mum went straight to see Ted.'

Pulling his eyes away again from obsessively watching the people spilling into the pub, David's eyes widened in alarm as he registered what I had said. 'You're kidding me! Did she explain anything to you before that?'

I felt a tight knot in my throat as I nodded. 'Some, little, nothing. It seems my Dad was not the Dad I thought he was either-'"

154

'So what's this surprise then, heh?!'

The loud obtrusive voice cut through what I was about to confide. We both swung our heads up to see Sean standing there, his wife holding back a little, her hand grasped tightly in her husband's. His leery grin left an uncomfortable, bristling feeling inside me.

'Don't tell me - you two are together .. duh come on, let's face it that was obvious from the moment we saw you-'

'Hello Sean .. Amy.'

Everything seemed to hush around us, still, like a series of rotating movie clips stuck on the same scene.

Sean froze mid sentence, staring at us. Amy turned around, gasped loudly, dropped Sean's hand as if it was on fire. Sean finally swivelled round, and seemed to just stare and stare at Natalie as she stood there immobile, a tray of drinks in her hand. She, in turn, was silently watching Sean, ignoring Amy completely.

It was David who broke it, standing to take the tray from Nat, encouraging them all to sit down.

'So surprise guys! We found her, we found Nat! I know you had your doubts but mate, how flippin' great is this?!'

The words were right, but somehow weren't. It was the tone, the bright note a little forced, if you listened real close. And I was. I stared at David, watching him in turn watch Sean very intently. As if he was analysing every movement, every outward sign, every word Sean would utter from this point on.

Everyone played their parts expected of them ...except Amy who seemed to withdraw further into herself with every passing minute. And I think I knew why.

Without doubt, despite or because of their awkwardness and constant furtive glances at each other, there was a definite *something* between Sean and Natalie. Existing, living, breathing...

But how long had it existed? For always...or reignited now in seeing each other again after such a long time apart? David had mentioned to me their closeness over the years. What did that mean

155

in reality, for this here and now when everything was suspended in time waiting to see what Natalie would do next? When Natalie was still trying to hide the fact her living, breathing four year old was asleep only a few streets away? It wouldn't be long before everyone knew who Lottie was, so why not mention her tonight amongst "friends"?

An unexpected moment came to talk to Amy alone. Natalie and Sean went to buy another round, and David was distracted talking to a friend on the table behind us. I looked across at Amy. She was staring after Sean and Natalie who were standing by the bar, heads bent towards each other, talking furiously. There was a half triumphant smile on Natalie's lips.

Concern swept over me for this woman beside me, clearly unhappy, anxious, vulnerable. Before my nerve and opportunity deserted me, I gently placed my hand on her arm, trying not to startle her, and clearly failing when she jumped like a startled deer.

'Sorry, I didn't mean to make you jump.' I apologised. Her features relaxed a little. I plunged on. 'I just wanted to see how you were doing, we haven't had much chance to chat...'

I let my voice trail off, hoping she would take up. Amy gave a strained little smile and the tiniest shrug of her shoulders in reply. Nothing more.

I tried a different tactic, a slightly more daring one. 'It must have been a shock just then to see Natalie appear like that, out of the blue.'

She stared at me, but the stare seemed to go right through me. It was a little unnerving. Her voice held an almost cold note to it, which shocked me to hear it, as she said, 'She shouldn't have done this.'

Done what? I was about to ask, confused, intrigued, but at that point David was turning around and introducing me to his friend. Amy looked away and the moment was lost.

David and I made our excuses first. I looked back to the three of them as we walked out. No-one was saying anything; the tension almost palpable. A small part of me wondered if we should go back. But David, who seemed very keen to leave as soon as possible, reached for my hand to give it a kiss, smiling down at me. I found myself all too easily falling into step with him, pushing them to the back of my mind so as to exist in the right here and now with David. I knew Mum was waiting for me back at Ciara's, she'd text me while we were having our drinks, and that we needed to talk tonight. So I would take this moment with all that I had.

As we headed out, Ciara came in. We smiled as we passed each other. Some inner instinct made me turn to watch her walk up to the bar, pause, wait for Greg to turn around to her. When he did, he looked thrown for a moment, vulnerable even, as he stared at Ciara, before his smile was thrown back on. I couldn't see anymore after that, as annoyingly my view was now blocked by punters heads. I frowned, frustrated. *Something is there between them, I'm absolutely certain of that.*

A moment was in fact all we did have; the short distance it took to walk me slowly back to Ciara's. David had invited me to his flat and I wanted nothing more than to go with him. The look in his eyes alone was persuasion enough. But I forced myself to shake my head regretfully, ruefully.

'I don't think it would take much to persuade me to take up your invite, but I can't.'

'I like a challenge to my powers of persuasion.' He grinned, a cheeky glint in his eye before pulling me into a kiss that held lots of promises.

When we finally pulled apart, I felt a little flushed but somehow still managed to say, 'Your powers are good ... very good- '

'Thank you.' He mumbled, stroking back my hair, giving me delicious goosebumps.

'But I still can't come to yours.' I breathed out, disappointment lacing my voice.

'Damn… I'm a broken man, cruelly rejected by the fiery English girl.' David lamented loudly to the open air in theatrical gesture. I laughed, pulling his face down to kiss him.

'Just don't tell my adoring fanbase about this, okay?' He gave me a severe warning look mixed with an adorable grin.

I smiled. 'I promise to take it to my grave.' I placed a solemn hand on my chest.

'Come on then, let's get you back to your mam like a good girl. I'm presuming you are going to introduce us?'

My eyes widened, a little excited, a little alarmed. 'I can, if you really want to meet her…'

'Of course I do. I'll grill her about your Dad and Ted if you like. See if my powers of persuasion can work better on the more mature lady.'

Seeing my aghast look, David gave a loud guffawing laugh, clearly amused by his own humour, before pulling me along the path.

Chapter Twenty One

Though she covered it well, smiling wide, I knew her well enough not to be fooled. Mum was completely thrown by this sudden scenario we were presenting her with.

'Oh.. my goodness ... David! How wonderful to see you ...last time I saw you you were much smaller.' She rose from the bed she'd been sitting on, her eyes falling to where our hands were linked, throwing me a dilemma. Should I let go? I felt sudden embarrassment, all too acutely aware of the newness of us and with it all the uncertainty and fragility that came with this. *I really should have said something before...*

David, in direct contrast, was charm persona, immune it appeared to any awkwardness, thank goodness. 'Mrs Crossways, it's great to meet you... again, I should say.' He turned to include me with a smile. 'Lily has been speaking highly about you. How are you finding our fair weather so far?'

'Oh! Um, good, thank you.' Mum turned to me, trying hard to keep up with events. 'So, you two are obviously close ...friends.'

I took pity on her. 'A little more than just friends, Mum.' I looked up at David, who nodded. 'Though we still haven't quite worked out what's going to happen when I go home.'

As I said the words, a physical pain gripped me. Beside me, David's smile slipped a little, as his hand tightened on mine. I swallowed hard, determined to hold it together. All too easily I could slip into melancholy, panic, or whatever it was you called this emotion stirring within me.

Mum, my beautiful mum, sensing all of this, smiled brightly at us both, her hands reaching out to touch ours. 'Don't worry, it will work out if its meant to be. Corny, but so true. You'll see. Now, I'm gasping for a cup of tea. Shall we see if that lovely Ciara is back and would like to join us for one downstairs?'

159

The delight I felt in having Mum and David together, laughing and relaxing over a tea and whiskey respectively, both strengthened and alarmed me. If only we lived here, came the maddening thought, over and over, then David and I could give this a chance to see how it grew, developed, without outside influence or time pressure heightening every thought, every moment. It was like a loud insistent alarm waiting to go off, its piercing sound giving no let up.

If I was meant to meet him, was it just to help him find his sister... or is this something more? Should I fight to stay with him?

With both Ciara and Mum beginning to yawn loudly, I reluctantly sent David out into the night.

We stood together in the doorway, heads close. I leant back against the doorframe. We gazed at each other, the silence charged with words we were both trying to form with neither knowing how to. Or even to begin to understand what this was between us - a fleeting holiday fling that had sprung up under extreme circumstances ... or something far deeper, far greater; a love that could build us a future together. A sustaining love.

'When does your flight leave?' David's eyes were searching mine as he asked the question.

'Later tomorrow.' I answered, unconsciously sighing.

'Just one day.' David's voice was low. He broke his gaze and looked down.I touched his cheek, drawing his head back up.

'We can't just leave it like this, not talking about ... about you going.'

'I know.' I sighed again. 'I know.'

'Tomorrow?'

'Tomorrow.' I tried to smile. His hands came down and cupped my face, pulling me into a hungry almost frustrated kiss, a hunger equally matched on my part.

Finally, we drew back. Without a word, David kissed me on the forehead then disappeared into the darkness.

I watched his figure be enveloped by the night, then slowly I shut the door, leaning my head for a moment against the door, trying to compose myself.

When I reached the top of the stairs I hesitated, looking first towards my door, then towards my mum's. With renewed determination I made my choice.

Mum was already in her nightdress. Somehow she seemed smaller, more vulnerable like that. If she was tired, which she must be, she hid it well, giving me a small smile, giving me the courage to draw in.

We sat together on the comfortable soft bed, talking quietly.

'So you and David seem very close, very comfortable with each other.' It was more of a statement then a question.

I stared at her. 'I think we are. But I'm so confused.'

'About what?'

I sighed deeply. 'About whether we are meant to be more, that we have a future together or is this just a fleeting holiday fling? Was I just there when he needed me, like a leaning post?'

'Have you asked him how he feels?'

I shook my head, biting down hard on my lip. 'I want to ... but I'm scared to. Does that make sense?' Mum nodded. I launched on. 'And even if he feels for me as strongly as I feel for him, how can this possibly work long term? Everyone knows long distance can't work.' I gazed at her hopefully, urging her to disagree, to say that love conquers all things and all of that make believe stuff we scoff at, but secretly yearn for.

But my mum, my pragmatic sensible mum gave a slight confirming nod. I felt a crushing sense of disappointment envelop me and swallowed hard to stop childish tears coming to my eyes.

'Have you not considered, though, moving here?' She cocked her head, gazing at me, as if studying me for the first time. 'You're different here somehow. Warmer, richer in emotion, more peaceful. I always felt you were scared of your own shadow, your own self,

161

afraid to let go and feel. But not now. You've emerged from that cocoon and if for nothing else, I have to thank David for bringing this out of you.' She reached across and took my hand as I stared at her. 'Its like you belong here. You've reached your destination, your resting place, just like your Dad did.'

'And you?' I whispered, searching her eyes.

She stared at me then turned her head away for a moment. 'I could, too easily. But its not so straight forward for me. I could devastate too many people and I can't live with that... I couldn't the first time.' She turned to stare at me. 'You can't build your happiness on someone else's misery. Ted and I both know that.'

'But you obviously both feel strongly for each other. Maybe if his wife knew that-'

'No.' Mum voice cut in strong, determined. 'He's not going to leave his wife for me. Nor do I want him to, that's not why I came back. I needed to lay some things to rest with Ted and we've done that. Marriage is a union, a selfless commitment to love the other despite all their faults, their weaknesses. It's about helping them to be all the person they're meant to be. I hope I did that for your dad, and I want Ted to do that for his wife. I believe in what marriage stands for and I want you, darling, to remember that too. Don't go into it lightly or with the belief they will be able to meet all your needs and emotions, because no-one can do that and you're just setting them up for a fall. I learnt that a little too late, but I know that you wont. So that's why, as hard as this is, Ted and I will have said goodbye again, both knowing that if one day he were on his own, and I was, then we'll find each other.'

I shook my head in admiration. 'How can you be so strong, mum? I don't think I have this in me, to let David go with such courage and selflessness.'

She suddenly smiled, her hand tightening on mine. 'You do, darling, you have it. But maybe you wont need to use it. '

162

I woke up determined to talk to David, to have the courage to tell him what I think he already knew; my growing love for him. I dressed purposefully, taking extra care in my appearance, all too uncomfortably aware the hours were ticking rapidly down.

I raced down the stairs, not bothering with breakfast, giving an open-mouthed Ciara a distracted wave as I flew out the door into the familiar streets, down the hill and into Main Street. I turned up the hill towards Cafe Peak..

As I did, my gaze fell towards the harbour as it had every day since coming here; wanting to briefly feast on my favourite view.

Only today, it would prove to be a fatal mistake.

Later, oh later I would curse myself for this innocent need. If I hadn't looked that way, if I hadn't set my gaze towards the far distant, if I had instead kept my head down and focused on my purpose.... then the awful turn of events that followed my innocent look wouldn't have become my undoing, my heavy weight to bear.

I froze, right there, wanting desperately to tear my gaze away, yet at the same time unable to do anything but stare. I found my feet cross over the road, pause unseen. My eyes watched, my heart thudded in my chest.

It was clear their conversation was agitated, passionate, one moment touching each other, the next turning away from the other. Their mouths were moving quickly, too fast for me to even try to hazard a guess as to what was being uttered.

I took one step; then another. As I did, my feet crunched on the stones, making me flinch with the loud sound.

It was loud enough for them to become aware of my presence, to both turn and be startled on seeing me; to give a awkward wave, as if this was all quite normal. They made no move to step towards me and I found myself hesitating, struck dumb.

'Nat? Sean? Is there something you need to share with us?'

The familiar voice of David's came from nowhere. My heart jumped and I spun round, momentarily distracting him from looking hard at Nat and Sean. 'Lil? I saw you heading over, then change

163

direction and I wanted to see what the sudden attraction was- Hey, stop, wait. You can't keep running away from this!'

Nat and Sean were already retreating, Sean shouting out, 'Sorry mate, Got to go. We'll talk later.' They hurried away. *Like cowards* came my grim thought.

David was staring after them, a strange expression on his face.

'Why wont they just come out and say it!!' He shouted to the careless air.

I turned his face to mine. I felt pale inside, buffeted almost. But I needed to stay strong for David.

'You know, don't you? Just like I've guessed. You've known it in your heart for a while, haven't you.' My last sentence came out as a statement then a question.

Angry sparks flew at me. 'Of course I know, Lily! I guessed from the first time Lottie smiled at me! I'm not stupid or blind, despite what they may think. But I don't want this to be the truth – can you get that?'

'I get that, I do. And they have to face up to the truth. No wait!' I forcefully stopped him from running after their ever growing distant figures. 'Let me go, okay? I'll talk to Nat.' As he started to protest, my voice took on a determination. 'Listen! I'm not family, so Nat will talk to me, I know she will. It was me she appeared to first and there has to be a reason for that. Maybe this is it, this moment!'

He stilled, turning to look at me. 'You can trust me.' I said quieter now, reaching up to hold him tight.

'Don't you think I know that?' He uttered a little desperately. 'Its just-'

I kissed him, smiled as convincingly as I could. 'I'll come and find you as soon as I can. I promise.'

I pulled away, quickly heading in the direction they went. My heart felt heavy, and my mind unprepared. I wanted to do anything but ask this of the girl who had only just been found, and could all so easily disappear again.

But I can't, I *won't* let David down.

Chapter Twenty Two

Where in hell were they?! You can't just vaporise like a ghost. Then again maybe that's exactly what you can do, when you're an expert at it.

I felt a rising sense of panic, and an immense feeling of circumstances starting to spiral out of my control. I swore repeatedly under my breath.

I was running up and down the different streets, my breathing laboured with the effort, my eyes scanning every person passing me. I couldn't shake the oddest feeling of eyes following my every move.

I found myself in a familiar road and paused to take stock. I looked across at the row of neat white terrace houses and suddenly it clicked. Iona's house!

Without pausing to think, I ran over to her door and knocked loudly, my body restless as I waited to see if anyone was there.

Just as I was about to knock again, the door swung open. Iona looked surprised for a moment to see me, taking in, with one look, my dishevelled self.

'Iona, hi, sorry to disturb you but I was looking for Natalie.' I gasped out, adding as strongly as I could. 'Its quite urgent.'

Iona shook her head a little ruefully. 'Sorry me darlin', I'm sure it is, but she's not here. Left quite early this morning... again.' She muttered darkly. 'Its just me and Lottie here. Poor girl needs to be in preschool but Nat doesn't seem to know how long she's staying for...'

I tried to smile. 'Okay, thanks. I'll keep looking.'

I made to move off. Iona voice pulled me back. 'I'm sure she'll be back any minute. And you look like you need some water. So why don't you come in now.' came the command.

I found myself obeying her, despite a moment of unease. It felt odd, disconcerting, being here in David's family home without him. I tried to push that aside, find my polite manners, say yes please to a cup of tea 'that would be even better in restoring you'.

165

As I followed her into the kitchen, Lottie jumped off the dining room chair from where she'd been sat drawing; pencils and felt tips scattered haphazardly across the table, a couple fell had fallen onto the floor beneath. I smiled at her as she shyly drew close to Iona.

'Wow, that looks good!' I said, pointing to the picture. 'What have you drawn? May I see?'

'Show Lily.' Iona encouraged with a nod. Lottie walked over to pick it up, then held it up from where she stood. I walked over and crouched down so I could have a proper look. It was hard to work it all out but I gave it a good stab.

'Okay, so let me see. You've got a sun, and is that a tree?'

She nodded, smiling a little now and suddenly her voice burst out to tell me more.

'Yes and that's some flowers here, see?'

'Oh, they're beautiful. And is that a girl there?' I guessed at the pencil thin figure with no arms, but did have two legs and lots of hair.

'Its Rapunzel and that's me there, see? And Maximus.' She added, pointing to a white rectangle shape with what must be his legs.

She had me stumped there. 'Maximus ? I'm not sure I've heard of him...'

'The palace horse, of course! He loves apples. Have you not watched Tangled?' Came the amazed voice.

I laughed. 'No, not yet. Is it good?' Lottie nodded enthusiastically, 'Maybe I can watch it one day soon. '

'You can watch mine if you like! Do you want to watch it now?' Lottie made to go and find it.

'Oh, I can't right now.' I hastily replied, feeling bad in letting her down. 'But I would love to watch it another time, if I can. '

Lottie's face looked crestfallen. I shot Iona a guilty look, and she came to my rescue.

'Why don't you put it on to watch it, anyway, while us adults natter?'

Lottie didn't need telling twice. She skipped off. Iona gave me a conspicuous wink. 'Not sure her mam would agree this early on in the day. But as grandma I'm allowed to agree to all the things we'd never have let our own children do!'

A few minutes later, we were sitting down at the felt-tip strewn table with mugs of steaming tea in our hands and the distant sound of Rapunzel in the background.

'So now, what's your plans? Are you staying on for longer?

Her bold question took me aback. But I guess she had every right to ask me; seeing as my appearance had literally shaken up her life.

I hesitated for a moment, undecided as to how much I should reveal.

'I … I don't think so. My flight is booked for this evening.'

My voice was laced in regret, confusion… and of course she picked up on that. Iona looked directly at me, calm, still. In contrast I was fiddling with anything my fingers could pounce on, my eyes avoiding her direct gaze. *I feel exposed.. and I'm not sure I like it.*

There was a silence between us for a moment. I daren't say anymore, for fear everything would come tumbling out.

'Lily, I know we don't know each other that well yet. But to be sure you've made an impact on this family.' There was a hint of laugher in her voice. It encouraged me to look up, match her smile. Her voice became more serious then. 'I may not have been grateful at the time, in forcing my hand like you did to find my daughter. But I am, darlin', I am, especially with this unexpected gift of a granddaughter.'

Tears pricked my eyes as she reached across and briefly touched my hand, before retreating back to her mug. I nodded, said softly. 'Thank you.'

'It's also quite obvious there's a connection, a... a bond that has grown between you and my son. Perhaps even love.' I felt my cheeks blush scarlet. 'It seems like you were meant to meet each other again, so long after first meeting as kids. And I'm sure that's the reason you clearly don't want to go.'

I felt a growing despair sweep over me, that I couldn't push down, not any more.

'I don't know what to do, Iona!' I blurted out. 'I've fallen for your son, but it's so complicated. The more rational part of me is saying put it down to a wonderful, but short lived romance, and return back to normal life. But another more daring part of me-'

'Is saying don't give up or walk away, yes?'

I nodded, my eyes pleading with her to give me the right answer.

Iona gave a little sigh. 'I'm no expert in this, God knows I've made enough mistakes, wrong choices. But one thing I've learnt is that every person comes into your life for a reason, a purpose. It may be for a short time, or it may be for your whole life and all you have is a gut feeling, a sensing of which direction it will be for that person. Go with your gut instinct, darling, God's given it to you for a reason.'

I stared at her, nodded. Her words spoke so deeply to me. I needed to hold onto them, mull them over.

We sat peacefully for a moment, sipping our tea. I was still on alert, praying yet dreading Natalie walking in through that front door. I decided to give it five more minutes.

'Did I see your mam in town? Or were my eyes deceiving me?'

I looked up, surprised. 'You remember my mum?'

Iona smiled. 'Vaguely, and I do mean vaguely, from years ago. We only met a couple of times when she came to collect you from our house where you played with Nat. I never forget a face, me, though must confess to forgetting her name...'

'Hannah.' I supplied.

'Of course! Of course I remember now! Is she just here for a holiday?'

I had to curb a smile as I acknowledged I was being superbly played into confiding in Iona. *She is good, very good,* I silently admired.

'Yes, to come and see me, catch up...' I let the sentence rest there, not wanting to reveal about Ted. Instead, I decided to ask the question burning to escape out. 'May I ask, did you know my Dad at all? Eliana, Greg's mum, seemed to think you did.'

Iona was caught in surprise at this. Her eyes widened, her hands stilled on the mug. 'Not really. I think I chatted with him a couple of times before he moved on, left Dingle.'

I greedily latched onto this. 'Did he say where he was going? When he left here?'

Iona frowned, as if trying to remember. 'I got the sense that he was just going to travel where the wind took him, so to speak. He seemed ... troubled. '

I stared at her, pressing forward in my seat. 'In what way?'

Iona was starting to look uncomfortable. I pressed in. 'Don't worry, I know about Dad's troubles here with the police. But please, anything more you can tell me to fill in this great big missing time in his life would help us so much. Mum and I never really knew why...'

Her eyes softened towards me, though she gave a helpless shrug. 'I got the impression from what he told me that it was money worries. I think he'd always had trouble keeping his spending in check, couldn't keep his head out of the water, as they say. Said he was too much like his own pa. That's why I guess he left you all, probably thought he was doing your mam and you a favour, though we tried to tell him that wasn't the case. Guilt can do funny things to you...But that's just my lasting memory talking here, I might have remembered it wrong.'

I closed my eyes, falling back, feeling the force of this new knowledge. The thought of my Dad running because he was scared, or troubled, sickened me to my core. What he did was wrong .. but how bad must it have been to act in this rash way? To be too afraid to meet our eyes?

'Sorry, me darlin'. Its probably not what you wanted to hear.'

I pushed a shaky hand through my hair. 'Its okay, I did ask.'

She gave me a pitying look, then went to stand up. 'Would you like another cuppa there?'

I shook my head, rising myself. 'No thank you. I should probably try and look again for Natalie.'

A sudden dark cloud swept across Iona's face. 'My daughter, unfortunately, doesn't always think though her actions, and what

169

effect they may have on others who love her.' She gazed across to where her granddaughter sat mesmerised in front of the film, before turning back to me. 'Whatever it is you have to tell her, Lily, promise me you'll make her sit there and listen to you. Don't let her run away. It's time she stopped running from the uncomfortable parts of life.'

I was back on the streets, Nat's mobile phone number clutched in my hand, with no real sense of where to go. I decided to try one more time searching, then if no luck head back to David.

I felt strange sense of surrealism as I now walked, like I had already glimpsed the future of this day and was merely fulfilling my part of it.

Half an hour passed with no sign of her. I let out a pent up sigh, refusing to dwell on the cowardly relief sweeping over me of not having to confront her.

As I rounded the walled corner heading back into Main Street, I nearly collided with a man clearly in a hurry. I gasped out loud and automatically grabbed the man's arm to stop us both stumbling. He looked down at me, annoyance and impatience sparking in his eyes. However, on recognising me, they widened in alarm.

'You knew she was alive all this time!' The words came rushing out of me, like a strong tidal wave I had no control over. 'How could you?! *You knew*!'

For a moment he went to deny it. I could see it in his face. Then, all at once, Sean's face crumpled up, as if the effort of all this lying had finally cost him something. His body slumped against the wall. His head slowly lifted and for a moment connected with mine then shifted away, as if looking too long into my eyes would condemn him on the spot.

'Yes.'

The word was uttered deeply, dragged up through him. One word, that told a thousand more. I stared at him, trying to mask my shock at his confession, at how life changing such a simple word could be. Still, I persisted in getting to the truth.

'All this time you knew where she was and you never told David, your supposed best mate, even though you witnessed what pain and heartache they were going through!'

He remained silent, refusing to meet my gaze. My anger now threatened to consume me. *How could you do this to him?!* My head screamed.

'Sean! Sean, look at me!'

For a moment he refused me. Then he finally raised his eyes to meet my own blazing ones. I saw defiance there. And something else I couldn't name right then.

'Tell me the truth, damnit ... are you Lottie's Dad?'"

Sean stared hard at me. I saw the fighting spark burn in his eyes, the almost nonchalant attitude that was far worse to me then denial. He gave a small shrug to his shoulders. 'You already know the answer to that, Lily, so why ask me?'

'Yes, yes I do.' I whispered, sickened to my stomach. I felt the overwhelming urge to get away from him. *Poor Amy. Poor Lottie.*

He suddenly grabbed ahold of my hands, throwing me off guard. 'You don't have to preach at me, Lily, or tell me how absolutely messed up all this is, what a crappy friend I am, a useless husband and a damn liar. ' He gave a humourless short laugh.'I know it, God I know it. And I can't fix this! It's too late now to stop any of it. The moment I've been dreading ...is actually here.'

His hands let go of mine, to drag his fingers through his hair. 'I love her, Lil, I've always loved her.'

This unexpected admission to real emotion had me stilling in an instant. I cautiously eyed him, not sure if he was playing me ... or finally telling me the truth.

'Natalie?' The name nearly stuck in my throat.

Sean nodded, his mind and thoughts dragging him far away. " Of course Nat. From when we were just kids, fooling around. But I realised it too late, like some damn fool, and now there's Amy in the middle of it-'

'Do you love Amy too?' The words burst out of me. I could hardly believe what I was hearing.

171

He turned to me. The new despair in his eyes threatened, for a moment, to shrink away my anger. I swallowed hard, refusing to feel sorry for him. 'I care about her, feel responsible for her. She's fragile... too fragile. You've seen her, you must know what I mean!'

I had, and I did know. I gave him a fierce look, feeling an icy feeling come over me at the thought of her knowing all of this. 'And who made her that way, huh?'

He ignored my accusation, too wrapped up now in his own self pity. 'She knows I love Nat, though I deny it.' He said, as if reading my thoughts. 'And she knows about Lottie. That nearly destroyed her as she's not been able to get pregnant herself. Before it was okay, because she never saw Lottie, never came with me to visit them in Cork. But now they are here in Dingle...' He gave another low moan, rubbing his forehead hard as if it would make this all go away. 'I want this to stop. I want this all to stop badly. I don't think I can live these two lives anymore. I have to choose.' His voice carried a pitiful note. He slumped down against the wall in a mess of self pity.

I stared down at him, at this sorrowful excuse of a man who had expertly played into the hearts of two women, all along knowing it would be the weaker one who would pay the price for their sin. I whispered in despair. 'Oh Sean, what have you done? What have you done?'

Chapter Twenty Three

'Sean? What are you doing?'

We both swung our heads up sharply on hearing the soft voice beside us. Sean slowly staggered back up to his feet.

Amy stood there before us, a local supermarket bag clutched in her hand. A confused questioning look was shot to the pair of us. I frantically tried to give her a semblance of a normal smile.

'Why aren't you at work?' She continued when she received no response.

Sean could only stare at her. *Come on, come on Sean, pull it together! You owe it to her!* I silently urged, just about refraining from giving him a physical shake.

To my relief, a brief false smile appeared, followed by a barely there laugh. 'I could ask you the same thing, darling. Why aren't you - how come you're here and not at the office?'

'Early lunch...' Her voice was quiet, unsettled.

I stepped in to try and ease the tension, forcing a jovial note into my voice. 'Hi Amy, I was just on my way to see David and literally bumped into Sean, nearly gave us both heart failure. Hence why he was on the ground!'

Amy stared at me then gave a little smile, as if in relief. Sean gave me a grateful look that set my teeth on edge, before putting his betraying arm around his wife to guide her away. 'Got something nice in there for my lunch?'

Amy smiled, besotted, allowing herself to be led away. I felt a strange heavy sickness in my stomach at seeing this; so insecure in herself she could only find happiness when Sean's attention fell on her.

'I have your favourite pasta sauce.'

'Mm sounds great-'

They began to walk away from me, and all I could do was watch them go.

'Sean! At last!!! Oh!'

The air stopped, held its breath, as we heard her voice followed by her; hand frozen in mid wave as she nearly collided with us.

To her credit, Nat recovered quickly, smoothing into her role. One warning shot from Sean was all it took for her to give a little laugh, lie easily; as if it had been played out like this many times before. 'I was just going to see if you were all free tonight for a drink, but don't worry, we can chat later!'

'Yeah, good plan. Let's do that. But my wife is going to cook me lunch now. ' His voice carried heavy emphasis. With that, Sean tried to steer Amy away. But this time she was not so easy to manipulate, as she took in first Nat with her over-bright eyes and flushed cheeks, then my frozen smile. It was a full minute before she allowed herself to be taken off.

Which left Natalie and I standing there, watching them leave. I felt an insane desire to laugh at the complete and utter disaster this all was.

Natalie avoided my eyes as she finally tore her gaze away from their retreating backs.

'Well, I should get back to Lottie-'

I reached out and grabbed her arm, hard.

'Not so fast! You're coming with me, right now, to see David. And you are going to tell him everything. The absolute truth.'

She turned and stared at me, her eyes sparking angrily. My eyes held hers with a steely determination. I was not letting her run from this anymore. Her face flinched as she saw her match in me.

At last she had the sense to look away, to give the barest of nods. I too nodded in reply. And together we walked in silence to David's cafe.

For a moment we stood there awkwardly, waiting for him to look up and see us. The cafe was still fairly quiet; not quite hit the lunch time rush, though to me it felt this day had been dragging on for many days. I was exhausted.

174

Then, David's head swung up from looking at his coffee order form. I sensed he hadn't really been focusing on it.

His eyes went first to Nat, then lingered longer on mine, seeking an answer from me to an unspoken question. My eyes must have held the daunting truth, for his own then narrowed and a grimness twisted his mouth.

I could sense the restlessness of my companion, no doubt fighting a desire to bolt. It was, after all, what her mind had trained her body to do. To be on the safe side I guided her over to the table I had originally sat at with David all that time ago when I first crashed into his life.

'There's something Natalie wants to tell you ... and you just need to listen.' I told him as firmly as I dared when he had come up to us. He sat down, nodding once. He crossed his arms. We both turned to Natalie.

Natalie looked at her brother, then gave a strange sigh. Her fingers tapped on the table. A defiant look appeared in her eyes, as if trying to convince us all that she was unperturbed by all this, that she had nothing to feel guilty about.

It didn't work.

'Okay, I'll tell you the truth ...but you're not going to like it, and I can't see how it will help anyone. Why do you think I've kept away all these years?'

David gave his sister a steely look 'Go on.'

Nat gave another sigh, followed by a shrug of her shoulders. She held her brother's eyes with a steely will I could not help but quietly admire.

'Sean ... Sean ... is Lottie's dad.'

She sat back after delivering this, crossing her own arms defensively. Her voice had been calm enough, but I could sense an underlying panic inside her of what David would say.

I turned to him, reaching out to take his hand. But he pulled away after a moment, a conflict of emotions flashing across his face.

'Just like that ... after all these years, you deliver this as if you were doing nothing more than telling me what the weather was like.

175

As if you don't credit me with having half a brain to have figured this out myself the minute I saw my niece? Nor that maybe I was just giving you the chance to come tell me yourself? *Is that it?!* That's all you are giving me after betraying me, Amy, mam-'

'Yes that's it! What do you want me to do, get down on my knees and beg forgiveness?!'

They had both now half risen out of their seats.

'Please! Sit down, let's talk about this in some semblance of calm!' I pleaded, trying to push them both down. They shrugged me off, ignoring my efforts.

'That would make a refreshing change, Nat! I can't stand what you've become -'

'Sorry to disappoint, brother. But I don't care what you think because he's the only man I really love!'

'Love? You call this love?! You don't even know how to love in any real sense of the word. And my own supposed best mate certainly doesn't.'

'How dare you judge me when you let your own fiancé down all those years ago!'

I froze, shocked to my core, my words to calm them falling silently away. Fiancé? What fiancé? My emotions contracted sharply, painfully. There was so much about this man I had yet to know, so many hidden locked away facets he had yet to trust me with. I slumped slowly down into my chair, unnoticed.

'Touché, Natalie. Touché. You know I hated hurting her knowing I didn't love her like I needed to-'

Whatever else he was about to say was cut by the loud shrill of his phone. He flicked it open intending to cut the call off but as he went to do so, his hand stilled. Very carefully, he pressed receive, put the phone to his ear.

It was only then I saw his sparks of barely controlled anger as he said, 'Sean.'

Nat gave a small gasp, standing up clumsily as David turned away from the table.

Something unexpected crossed David's features as he listened to fast frantic words being thrown at him. I stared at him, trying to gauge what had happened, watching the anger on his face being replaced by a deep frown.

'Where is she now?... okay, okay calm down ... we'll find her. I'll call you as soon as.'

'What? What is it?' Nat demanded breathlessly.

There was a grim look in his eyes as David said, 'It's Amy... she's gone missing.'

We all stood a little bewildered for a moment outside the café. I looked across at Natalie, while David spoke again to Sean on the phone.

For the first time, I saw a flicker of real concern and underlying fear for someone other than herself. That gave me hope; that underneath all of this cooler layers lay a heart that could be touched by human emotion. Perhaps now she would realise what her actions were doing - destroying the life of someone innocent in her determination to have Sean all for herself.

Love could be the most sustaining, wonderful gift given and received. It could help you to be all that you're meant to be. Selfless and fulfilling, in it's most purest and natural state. But it could also cripple you, bring you to your knees. Be utterly soul destroying, if one loves more then the other. It can turn you into a selfish, bitter person, demanding of it, wanting more than it can give you. All consuming. All destructive.

We have the ability to decide how to give it, how to receive it. We don't always remember this; this power we possess within us.

David came off the phone. 'We've agreed we'll all spilt up and look for Amy. If you see her text us immediately, so we can all find you.'

'Did he tell her?' Natalie asked breathlessly. 'Did he tell her he was leaving her for me and Lottie?'

David looked down at her and we saw the answer written in his eyes. 'I hope this makes you happy, sister.'

'Of course it doesn't-'

'Best thing we can do now is find her.' I interjected between brother and sister as they glared at each other. 'I'll head off this way.' I pointed to my right. 'You two go in that way. Keep your phones to hand.'

I physically pushed them off, which seemed to galvanise them. I watched them for a moment to make sure they were following my instruction, then started to jog the other way.

'Please God, please God,' I muttered as I jogged along, 'Let her be okay.'

What in fact was probably no more than ten minutes but felt like many long agonising hours later, I spotted a distant figure standing close to the pier's edge. Too close. It was clearly a woman and there was something strange about her posture. I quickly stepped closer, squinting my eyes to try and make her out.

The woman turned her head a little, and her profile was revealed to me.

It was Amy. I was sure of it. And now I knew why I had been sent on this journey, this path - for *this moment.* Not only to save Natalie from a life stricken with guilt, but to save Amy from herself. *But am I strong enough for this?*

I banged out a text to say where we were, just sending it to David who I knew would tell Sean and Natalie straight away.

Then, taking a deep shuddering breath, I walked carefully towards her.

My heart leaped a little in fear as I came near and saw how close she stood to the edge. She was muttering something under her breath, words lost to me in the wind sweeping up around us.

178

Although I had come quietly so as not to shock her, Amy must have sensed me for she spun round. I automatically reached out to grab her arm as her footing slipped a little. My heart raced even faster, anxiety and fear rushing right through me.

'Sorry, Amy. I didn't mean to startle you there.' I tried to keep my voice as calm as I could produce. 'I just wanted to see if you were okay...'

Amy stared at me, then gave a forced strangled laugh. 'Okay? Am I okay? What a question to answer!' Her voice rose to a high pitch, as she turned back round to look across the water.

'Listen, why don't we go and get a coffee at David's?'

If she heard she chose to ignore me, as she stared out across the expanse. 'Look how peaceful it is out there, so calm … yet it could suck me right down into its depths without a care or thought to me.'

My hand tightened a little further on her arm, though she tried to shrug me off. Her voice alone, strange and distant, was scaring the living daylights out of me. I took a discreet quick look behind me to see if the others were coming. No sign. I muttered a quick desperate silent prayer.

'That's true, it could.' I said, deciding to go with her thoughts. 'But only if we stepped too close to the edge. I think maybe we should step back a little-'

'Do you know the God awful sad truth about me, Lily?' Amy turned to me now. There was despair and self loathing there, making her eyes dark and tormented. Nothing before had ever had such a profound effect on me; as this did. 'I've been looking at this water, thinking how it could take me in, make all this pain and horrid feelings inside of me, here,' She stabbed her head. 'just go away. But I can't even do that! I can't even take a step over. What a loser, a failure. Just one step...' She turned to look again, her foot a little closer. 'Just one.'

I instinctively pulled us one step back again, and suddenly I was fighting hard for us both.

'Good! Because your life is precious Amy, its worth fighting for! Don't give up on it. I'm glad you can't take that step because that means you still have something inside you fighting to live. Do you understand what I'm saying to you? Do you?!'

Amy stared at me. Tears starting to fall from her eyes. 'I wish I was you.' She whispered in a heart wrenching voice, 'I wish I was strong, had faith like you do. I wish I was anyone but me. I'm not worth loving... they've taught me that.'

Tears stung the back of my throat. I pulled her hard into my arms. 'Don't say that, don't ever say that.' I whispered fiercely, 'You are worth loving, you are worth it, Amy.'

'Amy! Amy … come here darling. '

We looked behind us. There Sean stood, his face contorted in fear for his wife, his features strained. Just behind him was David, whose eyes connected with mine. He gave me a nod, a small smile of thanks. There was no sign of Natalie. *Thank goodness, thank goodness.*

Amy looked at me, desperate for reassurance. I smiled, gently let her go, nodded to encourage her towards her husband. He spread wide his arms, swallowing hard. Amy hesitated for a long moment then slowly walked towards him. He enveloped her with evident relief. I heard him saying again and again, 'I'm sorry, I'm sorry. I'll stay with you, I promise.'

I wish I could believe him came the unwanted harsh thought in my head.

It seemed to be all that Amy needed to hear though. Slowly, the stiffness left her body and she slumped against him, sobs racking her body.

After a few minutes, Sean started to lead Amy away. I felt a surge of relief course through me at seeing her move away from the edge.

I threw myself into David's arms, fighting back a wave of tears. His arms wrapped themselves around me and we both held each other tight.

I still do not know exactly what happened next, the chain of events still unclear, distorted with the blurriness of confusion maybe.

What I do know is that we heard Amy give a sudden cry - of anger, confusion, despair ... I still can't put a name to it. At the same time I heard Sean's voice shout out in alarm, 'No Nat!'

David and I sprung apart, spinning round. Before either of us could think or react, Amy eyes locked with Nat where she stood frozen, unsure, on the other side of the road to us.

Angry, despairing words were falling out of Amy's mouth as she yanked herself free from Sean's grip. I think I shouted out Amy's name as she blundered blindly into the road, hellbent on getting to Nat. I screamed her name again as I saw an unsuspecting car approaching her.

The screech of the tyres as the car hit her was the most horrific of sounds.

Watching Amy hit the bonnet, then fall down with a loud cracking thud onto the road's unforgiving surface, was the sound of nightmares cruelly colliding into reality....

Chapter Twenty Four

David took control, phoning for an ambulance, while stopping a shocked and ashen faced Sean from trying to move an unconscious Amy. Torturous minutes ticked by as we anxiously waited for the reassuring sound of sirens to fill the air.

At last! The paramedics sprung into action, carefully moving Amy onto a trolley then pushing her through the wide open ambulance doors, Sean all the while clinging to her side. David, meanwhile, had been trying to calm down the hysterical driver, and it took a few precious moments for the ambulance crew to persuade her to go with them in the second ambulance. They slammed the doors shut and flew off, its sirens still blaring; a sure sign that Amy was not in a good way.

David came over to Natalie and I. We stood there in a state of shock.

I'd always assumed I'd be okay in a crisis, having always been complimented on how calm and level headed I was. I thought I'd always be someone people could rely on.

But it appeared that I wasn't, not at all. Instead, I had fallen apart. I looked dazedly at David; who though pale was still steady. He took in our colourless features, our shaking hands, and without a word guided us both over to his cafe.

It was only when I found a hot sweet cup of tea in my cold hands and one of David's warm jumpers wrapped around my shoulders that I began to connect with reality, to take in what was happening. The cafe seemed to be empty; David must have closed it.

I looked across to where he now sat with Natalie, coaxing her to also take a mug of tea. She seemed to be physically shaking. David was rubbing her arms.

He must have sensed my steadier gaze because he looked up. At seeing my features returned to a more normal colour, he gave a soft sigh of relief and hurried over to me, crouching down to look deep into my eyes, assessing my state.

'How are you feeling?' He softly asked, touching my cheek.

I gave a little nod. 'Better, I think … I'm sorry I didn't help. ..' My voice began to break. 'Sorry I didn't stop this-'

'Hey, its okay.' David took the mug of tea out of my hands, then pulled me close into a hug. I pressed my face against the reassurance of him. 'It's not your fault, got it? You did more than any of us. Trust me on that.'

I clung to him, before he gently pulled me back, took my hands. 'Listen my darling, I need your help.'

I nodded, fighting to get my emotions under control. 'Okay.'

David smiled, unexpectedly. I felt my spirit lift in reaction. 'I need you to take Natalie back to mam's, look after her for me.'

'Where are you going?'

'I need to go to the hospital, I need to be there for them.'

'Of course you do, of course you do.' I nodded fiercely.

His eyes closed for a moment, weariness descending. 'What a mess, what a complete and utter crappy mess.'

I grabbed his hands, holding tight. 'We can sort this. Everything can be sorted.' I urged.

'I really hope your right. Let's pray you're right... '

Iona took one look at us and to her amazing credit, didn't ask any questions. She hugged her pale daughter to her for a moment then settled us down in the lounge before disappearing to make us 'a nice soothing cuppa, that's what you both need now.'

I looked across at Natalie as she sat huddled, as if her body was trying to curl into itself, shut out the world. She barely knew I was there and instinct told me to allow her to slowly force herself back into this world.

This took an agonising long time, where I literally had to clamp my mouth shut, before she finally turned to look at me. I knew then, as our eyes connected, that shock had finally left, had withdrawn from her, leaving behind realisation ... and humbleness. Nat's eyes held a resignation and recognition of the bitter truth. Was there even a touch of self loathing there?

'How are you feeling?' I gently asked her, moving slightly forward in my seat.

'A little better.' Her voice sounded hoarse, shaky.

We looked at each other for a moment longer then, suddenly, Natalie was crying, burying her head in her hands. I hesitated for the briefest of moments before human pity swept over me. I moved over, sitting down beside her then pulled her into my arms. I let the tide immerse her.

I heard footsteps, and looked up to see Lottie standing there uncertainly. Fortunately, Iona also appeared and quickly pulled her away, talking softly to Lottie as she did.

When the crying had lessened, I drew back so I could see Nat's face, braced myself then to quietly ask, 'Are you crying for Amy ... or for yourself?'

Nat looked startled for a moment, her defences almost rearing up. Then something happened as I forced her to return my stare... something crumpled within her, I think.

'For both of us.' She admitted, honestly. 'This is all so hopeless! So impossible. A total cock up, isn't it?'

'Yep.' I answered truthfully. A half laugh, half sob slipped out of Nat. 'But you know what you have to do. ' I continued.

Nat stared at me . 'I don't want to.' She whispered brokenly.

My heart contracted on seeing her despair, but I pressed on, surprising myself with my determination and hardness on her. 'I know. But you have to. He's not yours, he's never been yours. Can you see that now? He can be Lottie's dad, in fact he needs to be her dad. But that's all. That's all it can be. You've been given this gift of your daughter, don't take that for granted! Sometimes I think that we're all striving so hard to search for what we think we still need in our lives, we don't stop to appreciate what we already have. Let Lottie be enough for you, please. '

Tears escaped from her in a rush. I took her hand.

184

'I know, I know.' She forced out. 'I have to walk away, I know. But why? Why me to walk away? It's not fair-'

'You can do this, Nat.' I fiercely replied, ignoring her self pity, trying a different tactic. 'I see a strength in you, a determination that I can only admire... and that's why I know you'll do this, walk away, go to Amy and ask for forgiveness for what you and Sean have done...'

Her head began to shake violently at this, panic coursing through her. 'Please, don't make me do that! I will leave with Lottie today, but I can't do-'

'Look at me, Nat.' I commanded. Finally her eyes reluctantly did. 'Amy deserves nothing less and it will bring closure for you all. You must make this right, for your sake as well as hers. In case there's not another chance. In case Amy doesn't...'

The words hung in the air for a moment, its meaning heavy and subdued. Even though I heard myself saying those words I was full of doubt if any of this was impacting on Natalie.

So when I heard her say, 'Will you come with me? To the hospital?' I could only stare. I think she feared I was about to say no to her, for she grabbed my hand hard and her eyes pleaded with mine. 'I can't do this alone. Please help me. Help me make this right.'

At last my question had been answered as to why she had appeared to me in my photo all those weeks past ... for such a time as this. I let out a long releasing breath. I think my journey had nearly reached its end point, and right then I didn't know how to feel, how to react.

But it wasn't the time to think about me. I nodded, smiled a little. 'Of course I'll come with you. '

Why were hospitals so stifling? I fought against the urge to escape back into the fresh air as we walked through the doors of Dingle's Community Hospital.

We eventually found our way to the ward where Amy was. We stopped outside the small offside room they had put her in. A shiver

185

went through me as I saw her lying there, small, motionless, with too many drips and tubes attached to her.

Inside the room, David looked up from where he stood behind Sean, and physically started in seeing us both standing there. He said something to Sean, whose head swung up sharply. He stared at Nat, then gave a brief nod as David pushed through the door to us.

'I hadn't ... expected to see you both here.' He said as he kissed first me, then Nat on the cheek.

'There's something Nat wants to say to Amy.' I explained in a rush, trying to silently plead with David to go with this.

He seemed to understand, or at least trust me enough not to question it further.

'How .. how is she?' Nat's voice was quiet, small as she stared through the window.

'It actually looks worse then it is,' David hastened to reassure us, 'The tubes are there just because she's in an induced coma till the swelling in her brain goes down, which should be in the next day or so, then they will bring her round. The doctors are pretty confident no long term damage has been caused. Apart from a few broken ribs nothing major has been damaged. She's lucky, really lucky when you think what could have been..'

I closed my eyes in relief, leaning into David for a moment. 'Thank God.'

'That's good. That's really good.' Nat said, a small smile appearing for the first time. She turned to us. 'Would it be okay if I went in for a few minutes?'

She was already opening the door without waiting for a reply. I touched her arm. 'Do you want me to come in with you?'

She briefly smiled, touched my hand. 'I need to do this alone.' Taking in a deep breath, Nat pushed open the door.

David and I stood with our arms around each other, each unconsciously holding ourselves still.

We watched Sean jump up from the chair. I watched them quickly embrace, then Nat walk over to Amy and take her hand. I saw Sean take a couple of steps back, huddled up in himself, as he stuffed his

186

hands into his back jean pockets. I wanted to believe that this would be a turning point for Sean, that he would accept responsibility for what he had driven Amy to. I wanted to think that somewhere inside of him, there still lingered a good part. Yet ... yet something in his manner, in his stepping back from his wife, from not confessing together but instead letting Nat take the blame alone, told me my hope was as certain as snow falling in June.

My eyes watched intently as I tried to lip read what Nat said to Amy for those next few moments, though had a strong sense of what they may have been. I do know it made Sean turn away, unable to watch. Nat give Amy a quick kiss on her cheek before slowly turning to Sean, open unashamed tears on her face now. At that point, we both mutedly turned away from watching. It felt wrong to intrude.

David held me closer, kissed me on the crown of my head.

'I never expected our last few hours together to be like this ... anything but this, you know?'

My head swung up to look into his face. The sadness there spoke more powerfully to me then the words he was trying to tell me in his own slightly awkward way.

'I'm not quite gone yet, we still have ...' I groped to see my watch and my spirits dropped in despair, 'three hours or so.' I had to breath deeply, control myself. David seemed to be struggling a little himself as he swallowed a couple of times. 'We still have three hours.' I repeated, 'Do you think you can leave here soon?'

'Yes, yes.' He fiercely replied, taking my hand. 'Without doubt, I'll find you.'

I nodded, biting my lip. 'I'll wait for you at Ciara's until the very last minute I can.'

The door swung open, startling us both.

Nat stood there, sombre but collected. I admired her for that; this inner composure. She looked at us both, then calmly said, 'Lottie and I need to go home now. We need to go back and start over. Just the two of us.'

David pulled her quickly into a hug. 'Just promise me you wont turn into a stranger again.. I don't think I could bear that a second

187

time. Come and see us, talk to us, let us come and visit.' His voice was thick, vulnerable, protective.

Nat clung tight to him for a moment. 'I wont do that to you again.' I heard her whisper, 'No more hiding, I promise. I don't want to lose you again either.'

I gave them a little longer then gently took Nat's arm. 'Come on, I'll give you a ride back to your mum's.' I turned to David. 'I'll see you shortly?'

Why don't I want to leave your side? Am I fearful this is my goodbye to you already? With the best will and intention on your part, can you really make it? Can you? Are you meant to get to me or am I being spared from a painful goodbye?

'I'll be there. Wait for me.'

Chapter Twenty Five

I found myself upon its calm sandy surface, its draw to me as strong as ever despite every passing minute ticking loud and insistent in my head.

But I needed its sense of calmness and serenity today, more than ever. I needed to say goodbye to it, as odd as that sounded. And to say thank you, thank you from the deepest part of my heart - for releasing me, for freeing me from the strangleholds I had imprisoned on myself, for giving me the courage to come here and find Natalie... For giving me David. For leading me to love...

I know, I know, my ramblings and thoughts may seem crazy and illogic. Fanciful even. But for once, I just didn't care. I wanted to shout out loud, 'Thank you, God!' and dance about wildly.

I didn't though, I hadn't quite reached those levels of abandonment. So instead, I contented myself with drawing, on the sand, mine and David's initials within a heart, smiling shyly at myself for doing something I would have scoffed at a few weeks back.

A border collier, wet and shiny in the sun, came bounding up to me, woofing and offering me a rather chewed, wet stick. I gave a laugh and stroked his eager head before his owner whistled for him, giving me an apologetic smile as he did. The tongue hanging dog raced off, my eyes following him.

As I stared something strange happened within my mind - the man and the dog evaporated and instead I saw a vision of my dream from a couple of weeks ago. I was standing on this beach, wearing my flowery shorts and clutching my bucket in my childlike hand. My three friends were running towards me, as before. Except this time I clearly recognised their faces as they were now – Natalie, Greg and David.

'Where have you been?' Demanded Natalie, her voice high, her hair whipping around her. 'Come on, we've found a small cave. Dave found it and he's letting us go with him!'

With grins and laughs the three were turning, Greg and David the faster of the three, so trailing Natalie behind. She turned and waved at me, beckoning me to come.

As before, I stayed immobile, unable to move from my spot. But instead of feeling trapped, panicked as before, this time I felt a peace settle over me. I watched the children run further and further away from me, until the boys became just specks in the horizon. Natalie was walking away now, her back to me.

I let them go, and I let my child self go with them.

As I accepted this, smiling a little, Natalie seemed to grow taller as she moved away … until she become her present height and look. I started at this mesmerising hallucination, wanting to shake my head to bring myself back to normality, to the real world. Yet, somehow I felt I needed to wait, just for a moment, to see what she would do. Would the haunted look still be there as it had been in my photo?

Holding my breath, I willed her to turn around, so I could see her face just once. Something deep within me wanted, *needed* to know this Natalie was okay, she would be okay. Her face had caused me to literally drop everything, risk everything safe in my life to rush to her. Now I needed some release. I needed assurance, a sense of closure, before I left this beach, and this country, today. Before I had to leave behind her brother; not knowing if I would ever see him again…

I found myself rising onto my toes so as not to lose sight, my heart pounding, my fists clenched by my side as I whispered aloud, 'Turn round, please turn round.'

Her figure was growing more and more distant, and my mind was starting to pull me back to the here and now, to shake the picture away. I fought back hard, straining to still see her.

And then, with my breath catching, Natalie slowly spun round. Our eyes locked. I strained with all that I had to still see her features, as they threatened to fade away.

190

And then, and then at last - a smile broke across her face! Just for a moment before she turned away, until she vanished completely. But that was enough for me.

A strong primal instinct had me then pulling out my laptop from my rucksack, which I had grabbed from the car, and one final time open up the photo that had pulled me in every which way possible and radically changed my life forever. I think something in me already knew that when I looked at the photo this time, Natalie would be gone. Yet still I gave a soft gasp as I stared at the serene idyllic photo of Iona beach, deserted of people, exactly as it had been when I first took the shot all those weeks back. No haunting woman's face stared desperately at me; not any more, not ever again.

I let out a deep shuddering half sob, half laugh. Relief coursed through me. I was free, I was free! I couldn't explain it, definitely couldn't rationalise it, but I knew it was real, these feelings were real. Now I could let Natalie go, let this huge responsibility go. She would be okay. We would all be okay.

I should say goodbye.

I stood looking across at the now familiar pub's facade, half torn between rushing back to the B& B to ensure I'm there for when David arrived... and doing the decent thing.

The decent thing won. After all, I still had time on my side. Just.

As I crossed over to its welcoming threshold, I stole a look at my watch. I had just under two hours left. What I wouldn't give to be able to double, even triple that time.

But face reality, girl, no matter how long you had left, you'd still be standing here in this exact same spot, bracing yourself to say your goodbyes.

A sigh rippled through me. Then I looked up.

Greg isn't here! I scanned the room and every inch of the bar, twice just to make certain, but he wasn't standing in his usual spot behind the bar.

I quickly walked up to the new to me grey- haired, serious looking bartender, who was pouring a pint for my two friends sat hunched over in their normal places. I gave them a wistful smile, before turning to the bartender.

'Hi, is Greg around?'

He looked up, gave a shake of his hand with a small polite smile. 'Sorry no, he's had to go out to the old cash and carry. Can I help?'

I shook my head. 'No, its okay. Don't worry.'

'Why you lookin' so glum in the mouth then, lass?'

I looked across to these lovely old men and tried to smile brightly. 'What makes you think I'm glum?'

The two of them pulled comical faces. 'Well now, your chin is practically touching your shoes for a start.' the other one commented.

I couldn't help laughing, then sobered as I explained. 'I have to go home today.'

'And you don't want to go.' Finished the taller of the two. 'Now that I can understand. Its beautiful place here, that's for sure.'

'It is, it really is.' I hastily agreed.

'But its not the place really that makes you sad leaving. It's that fella you love, right? Our Greg-'

The smaller one butted in before I could say anything. 'Don't be daft, man! It's the coffee shop man you love, isn't that right?

'I wish it had been me... but there's the breaks.'

The unexpected voice from behind startled us all. I spun around to see Greg standing there, a funny little smile on his face as he looked at me.

'Greg!' I gasped, 'I'm so glad you got back... so I could say goodbye. Properly.'

I found myself throwing my arms around him, holding him close. That maternal need to protect him from knowing the truth about our parents still consumed me. I wanted him to remain innocent of it all.

After the smallest of hesitation, his arms held me tight for a long minute, then pulled away.

'When do you head home?' He quietly asked me, looking away for a moment.

'In the next couple of hours.'

Greg forced a smile to his lips, clearly trying to be upbeat for my sake. I quickly returned the smile, grateful for his effort, feeling awful I had caused him unnecessary pain and hurt.

'So just time for a last quick one, in a manner of speaking, of course.' He added in that old cheeky way I remember.

I grinned, relieved, knowing he was going to be okay. Of course he would be okay. 'Always got time for a quickie... for my new "brother."' I chirped back, hoping somehow he would understand what I wasn't verbally saying, and what we could still be to each other; platonically.

'Well, if you're offering,' My old friends cut in, a twinkle in their eyes as Greg gave a surprised but genuine smile, 'it would be rude of us to turn you down...'

'Oh go on then, pour them an extra one.'

As Greg poured our drinks I found myself watching him, chewing my lip as I inwardly argued whether I should raise Ciara's name with him. *Well, it is now or never,* and somehow that thought made me bolder then I normally would be.

'There you are, enjoy 'cause you wont get a drink poured so well in little ole England, english girl.'

As I reached across for my iced cold drink, my fingers caught and trapped his to stop him from moving away, taking him by surprise.

'Tell me to mind my own business,' I rushed out, 'But I can't help having this really, *really* strong feeling that there's something between you and Ciara ... Or was.' I continued, trying hard to gauge the stare he was currently giving me, to get some kind of confirmation I was on the right path here.

Or not... Greg was saying nothing, giving me nothing. *Oh heck, darn it and everything else. Might as well plough on now. Even if my cheeks have gone their cursed red.* 'Only if I'm right then I think, and can see, that whatever it was or is... is still there between you. I've seen the way she looks at you, the pain in her eyes when she saw us coming back from our date. I know what that means for a woman.'

193

That got to him, hearing Ciara's hurt, for he was gripping me fingers a little painfully now and there was something real, something which had moved him showing in his eyes. Hope maybe?

'Are you sure you saw that, Lily? Pain in her eyes?' Greg leaned closer, his eyes boring into mine. 'Because this is serious, to me, to even go down that road again, to even think of her.' He looked away and when he turned back I felt my heart contract for him when I saw the same pain in his eyes. 'She pulled away from me, not the other way round. I'm not sure I can lay myself open to her again. Once was enough.'

Suddenly he was pulling away from me, the shutters starting to close over. I physically yanked him back.

'I'm not sure why she did; walked away from you I mean. But I know Ciara and there must have been a very good reason for it. Don't write her out of your life, not yet.' I urged, 'Talk to her at least, have that conversation that maybe you've never had. I would give anything to be staying here with David. You two are *right* here, in the same town, across the street from each other, literally, and you could be on the verge of something so right, so amazing together! Please, please just talk to her.'

I was fighting back tears and trying hard to control them. I knew I was not as impassive as I should be, knew I was as much fighting against circumstances with David and I, as I was for Greg and Ciara. But the fact still remained - Greg and Ciara; theirs was a story only halfway through its pages.

Greg held up his hands as if shielding himself from any more verbal assault. 'Okay, okay, I will think about talking with her, no promises though.'

I broke into a smile, gave him a kiss on the cheek, swallowed down some of my drink then regretfully said goodbye.

I raced up the hill and almost crashed through the door into Ciara's. The lady herself looked up in surprise, then smiled. I smiled back, though had a bad feeling it wasn't quite reaching my eyes.

Ciara put down the bundle of warm pressed sheets held in her hands and came up to me.

'I'm going to miss having you here.' She pulled me into a hug; fierce almost in its swift intensity. I hugged her back, before we both pulled back.

'You've been amazing, Ciara. I've felt so at home here. Thank you for helping me and not ... you know ... thinking I was crazy trying to find Natalie.'

Ciara laughed with sweet abandon. 'Well now, you've come to the right place to do crazy things ...we're all a little crazy here, would you not say?!

I grinned. 'Maybe just a little. Ciara, has David been here yet? Or called?'

Ciara gave me a sympathetic look. 'Not yet. Don't worry, as soon as he does I will shoo him up to you quick smart. Your mam is packing upstairs.'

I gave a sharp intake of breath, sudden guilt washing over me. In the whole of this day's event I had completely forgotten my poor mum, who no doubt was having the same gut wrenching feeling of having to say goodbye... only for her once again.

As Ciara went to move away, I found myself doing the same to her as I had just done moments ago with Greg - I physically pulled her back. I couldn't let her slip away without confronting her with her feelings for Greg, hoping against hope that if they were both prepared and open with the other, they would finally stop being stubborn and just *talk*. Their hearts were already ripe for new beginnings, for deeper love this time - they just needed to realise that for themselves.

'Is there something you still need before you head off?'

'Ciara, I'm going to say the same thing to you that I've just said to Greg and you can tell me afterwards to butt out-'

'Greg?! What do you-'

I carried on, ignoring her as I fixed her with a firm look. 'I can see that you're both still full of feelings for each other, but neither of you are acknowledging it. And I know from what Greg's told me,' I quickly carried on as I saw her go to protest, 'that he's hurt from you walking away, wary of getting too close to you. But I don't believe for one minute that you two are over and done with, in fact anything but from what I've seen. So, please, for the love of everything, go and talk to him, be honest with what went wrong, and tell him how you still feel. You don't know how much I envy you, the chance to work this out, build a future together if you just let yourselves.'

I broke off, expecting to be told to stop interfering. Instead I was startled to see tears come into the eyes of the usually cheerful and constant Ciara.

'I hurt him so much, leaving him.' She confessed, her voice barely above a whisper.

'Why did you leave him?' I gently asked.

'I was scared, by how much he loved me. I thought I couldn't match it, would let him down.'

'And now? Do you still feel that?'

She stared at me, realisation hitting her. 'I don't think so, I think I'm capable of loving him as he deserves. Losing him has taught me how much I need him. Does that make sense?' I nodded, understanding completely. 'There's a chinese proverb that I'm just beginning to fully appreciate. It says "A life lived in fear is a life half lived". Maybe its time we both stopped living in fear.'

Once more, with eyes now filled, I nodded. 'Yes, yes I think you're right.' I breathed out.

Mum was leaning over her suitcase, her back to me as I rushed in without pausing to knock.

'I'm so sorry, Mum.' I breathlessly told her, 'Its been crazy, actually awful day which I'll tell you about in a minute. But anyway, I totally forgot to call or text you to tell you where I was. Are you okay?' I glanced down at her suitcase. 'All packed I see.'

Mum had turned to me by now, brushing her hair back off her face and giving me an amused patient smile that only a mother can produce. 'Yes, and I made a start on yours.. as time was pushing by somewhat fast.'

I purposely avoided looking at my watch, as if by doing so I could actually slow time down. *You're a foolish girl, Lily. No-one but God can do that.*

'We don't need to be leaving for another hour … I'm waiting to say goodbye to David.' My voice caught on his name.

Mum came and took my hand, sitting us down and said mildly, 'I must admit I'm half expecting to travel back alone. Have you two talked about you staying here more permanently?'

I gave a half smile, trying not to be taken aback by the directness. 'Of course I've thought about it. But neither of us have actually said it out loud. I still have no idea how David really feels about me.' I shook my head. 'I can't put my whole life on hold for anything less than the real thing on both our parts.'

Mum was silent for a moment, then looking down and stroking my head soothingly until at last she said, 'You've always been so cautious up till now with who you let close, who can touch you here.' She pressed her hand against my heart, 'even with me. No, no it's true,' She quickly continued as I began to protest. 'I know you love me, even if you find it hard to show me. I'm not the most demonstrative or love conquers all kind of woman myself. If I was, perhaps I would have taken the chance even now to stay for Ted... But darling, like I said before to you, since you've met David something has happened to you, something profound. It's like he's unlocked the real you, the real Lily who has an amazing capacity to love and be loved. Not in a needy way, but in a strong, graceful way. So you listen to me ,Lily." Her voice became fierce, strong as she cupped my face. I nodded, unable to speak; my throat thick and constrained. I've never heard my mother talk this way before, so open and emotional. 'If David comes tonight and if he shows you he has feelings for you, even just a little for now but which can grow into more, then you grab it with both your hands and you stay here with him and see where this new life takes you. I don't believe it's random, all of this. You're here for a reason.. and maybe that reason is David.'

'And if he doesn't feel the same?' I forced myself to say.

'Then you say goodbye, gracefully, with your head held high, thankful for all you have learnt by being with him and knowing you are now ready to be loved by someone else.'

I looked down, distraught at the thought. 'How can I say goodbye? How can I love again? It can't be that easy… you must know that more than anyone with having to say goodbye to Ted yet again-'

'Exactly, and if I can do this then you can definitely do it too. We're cut from the same fabric, after all.

Mum was smiling as she brought my face back up. She reached across and pressed a kiss onto my cheek.

Chapter Twenty Six

Mum and I had been waiting downstairs for the last ten agonising minutes. I couldn't keep still and was wearing the patterned carpet out from pacing up and down over it. Mum and Ciara, sitting calmly on the armchairs placed for guests comfort, kept casting me glances which I was studiously ignoring, as too the clock telling me we were already fifteen minutes late in leaving.

Please come, please come, David.

Mum was starting to make noises about making her own way in a taxi, so she could book us both in. I couldn't think straight to even reply. A knot in my stomach gripped painfully.

Mum carefully stood up and pulled her coat on. Ciara also stood and went over to the phone to ring for the taxi firm. I could hear her soft murmur as she requested a taxi from "Ciara's Bed and Breakfast" to Kerry airport. I tried to deafen it out, continued my pacing, glancing again at the clock as if I could will the minutes backwards. It clicked stubbornly on, the minute hand on a constant turning forward. I felt like going and yanking it off the wall. Instead I turned myself away from it.

A knock at the door! I flew to it before Ciara had time to even move, my heart pounding wildly, flinging it wide open, words already forming on my lips-

Only to fall away in sharp disappointment.

Greg stood there, and looked as taken aback at seeing me as I had in seeing him.

'I thought you would have already headed off. ' He said, thrown.

I just about managed a shake of my head, biting down on my disappointment, my despair. 'No, not yet.' I couldn't say anymore, my voice had grown thick.

Not that it mattered, Greg hardly noticed. He was too busy staring at Ciara.

She finished her call in a bit of daze, slowly replacing the receiver.

'Greg?' Her voice held a questioning surprised note to it, as she took one step towards him. She seemed to suddenly come alive as he in turn took one step closer to her, closing the gap a little, yet still far from each other. 'Are you okay? You … haven't come here in a long time.' Her words hung suspended in the air.

'I feel like we need to talk .. at least I need to talk. Can we?'

Ciara bit her lip, and I could see emotion swimming just below the surface. Then she nodded. 'Yes, yes for sure, we can do that.'

Mum and I glanced at each other, then discreetly turned away as Greg followed Ciara into the lounge, his eyes fixed on her back before closing the door firmly after them. I felt my heart contract with hope and delight. *Oh, let them work it through* I breathed out.

'Would you like a drink or something?' I could hear Ciara offering, falling into her hostess role, her safety net.

'No, no, I'm good.' Greg was replying in a rush, his voice holding an urgent note. 'I don't really know how to start this conversation. I never thought I would be having it with you. But Lily seems to think there's something still there between us, that you regret our break up. Is that true, Ciara, because I really need to know...'

There was a long agonising pause, before I heard her breathe out, 'Yes, yes its true.'

I was determined not to eavesdrop anymore, even though their voices were quite clear and their tone urgent. To be honest, my mind couldn't totally tune in to them as I continued my agonising pacing. But I could hear Greg's continued low passionate voice, Ciara's soft urgent one … and then a sudden burst of laughter. And that's when I found myself breaking into a smile, for a moment forgetting my own pain. Laughter was good, surely? It broke the tension, allowed you to break down your barriers, step closer to each other. Bring a glimmer of light and hope back into your heart.

Just for a moment, I felt the bubble of excitement … Then reality began to seep back in, my mum's voice penetrating me as she asked me what I wanted to do. What I wanted ...*wasn't it obvious for crying out loud?!*

Don't leave me hanging like this, never knowing... Come on David, come on.

My feet continued to do their relentless pacing. Mum passed me my coat, which I reluctantly took but didn't put on, as if to defy it. I tried to ignore her checking her bag for our tickets, then walking over to the window as we heard the distinct sound of a car pulling in, signalling the arrival of our taxi.

I walked towards the door to go and tell the driver to please wait for a few more minutes to see if we needed him.

I never got the chance.

The door suddenly swung open, almost knocking me over with its force.

And there David stood, his hair a little wild, his voice rushing out an apology I didn't hear nor needed to.

The relief on seeing him physically there, filling up the air around us, made me throw myself into his arms, hold him tight.

And never want to let go.

Chapter Twenty Seven

It couldn't be any more unromantic; Ciara's dining room laid up with her stylish white dinner set ready for breakfast tomorrow. The lights overhead blazed bright over us.

We sat at my favourite table overlooking the bay. David pushed aside the plates and cutlery so he could reach for my hand. His eyes and face, it seemed, were full of things he wanted to say but like me, with the pressure that I had to leave any minute, rendering him as frustratingly mute as I was.

Then all at once a stream of words suddenly burst out of my mouth, without any premeditated thought. Each word was filled with a passion and an intensity I had always thought was beyond me...

'You know, when I came here I thought it was to help your sister, to find her for you and your family. But you know what, I think that it was me, actually, who needed to be found, to be saved. I needed this journey, I needed to be shown that I was capable of feeling and caring so much more than I ever believed I was capable of. That I'm stronger, and more courageous then I ever thought. And impulsive! I certainly didn't know that about myself... '

I gave a short laugh. David smiled a little, his eyes never leaving me. I reached across with my other hand to cup his cheek. Every part of me wanted to stress to him how vital, how liberating loving him had made me feel. My voice was full of determination as I cried out

'Don't you see, you're the key that's unlocked all of this!'

I gave a slight bemused shake of my head. 'I feel more for you then I've ever felt for anyone. I care more for you then I care for myself right now. I know this is love, real love. And I'll always thank you for that. Even when I am crying myself stupid on the plane and wanting to be back in your arms, I'll still be thanking the stars and heaven above for bringing you into my life.'

Before David could react, before I lost all resolve and begged him to ask me to stay, I stood, pulling him up with me. Then I reached up to give him a final kiss.

It was a kiss like no other. Even if David could never tell me how he felt deep inside, his kiss and touch did. I could feel him tremble a little, then reluctantly pull back so he could say something. He was shaking his head in disbelief.

'This has all been so crazy, so intense from the first moment you literally crashed into my life... And it hasn't stopped, not even today. I haven't had time to stop and think like I want to and now -n ow you're going and its making me think crazily, rashly. I don't want you to go like this ...'

These last words were almost whispered. He bent to rest his head against mine.

'I know, I know.' My words tried to comfort him, as I ran my fingers through his hair. 'It will be alright, you'll see. You'll be stronger now, knowing your sister is okay.'

'It's not just having my sister found. *You* have made me stronger.' His voice was fierce now as he locked me with his gaze, cradling my face. 'You've helped to restore my faith, my belief that there is a God who cares.'

'I'm glad.' I closed my eyes, then pulled him into a tight hold. His arms almost crushed me.

'I have to go, Mum is waiting...' My voice sounded far away, as if being spoken by another, not me.

He let me go. I wanted to shout out - *Why? Don't you get it, I don't want you to!*

Keeping my gaze averted, knowing already they were full of tears, I grabbed my coat and bag and started to walk slowly, so slowly towards the door. With every step I forced myself to keep going, reminding myself of what mum said - to only stay if he asks, if I was certain his feelings were as strong for me as mine were for him. My gut instinct had thought they were, but perhaps I'd been mistaken ... *because he was letting me walk away.*

Keep walking, just keep walking, keep remembering how much you've changed for the better. Its not been for nothing, it will never be for nothing.

You'll go on from this. It's just going to hurt badly for a while.

I reached the door. My hand stretched out and grasped the handle. I began to turn it, my heart heavy.

'Wait! Lily, wait! For the love of all of things!'

I froze. Was I dreaming this, hallucinating what my heart so desperately wanted to hear?

So unsure was I, I found I couldn't even turn around in case disappointment would flood me. So there I stood, immobile, a little silly, waiting to hear more. ..

And now his words were tumbling out in a crazy manner.

As I listened, my body began to sag in relief, my heart jump wildly, and a crazy smile splash across my face that only the door was a happy witness to.

'I know you would be giving up everything... and I mean literally *everything* in your life to stay here with me. I mean, even by Irish standards that's damn crazy. And I know I'd only be gaining by having you stay. Believe me, I know all this and I think that's what's been stopping me till now saying something. But seeing you then about to walk away and knowing I'll probably never see you again – I don't even have your email address, for crying out loud – something just literally broke inside me...'

I heard his steps come a little closer, his voice grow deeper with a beautiful sincere note I couldn't doubt for one second. 'I don't know what the future holds for us, I can't make you wild promises I might not be able to keep. But what I can promise you is this... that what I feel for you is real, that I'll be faithful to you in this, and give us everything I've got. That I'll never take for granted all that makes you *you*, nor what you've already given me and will keep on giving. I don't know what else I can say except that if you feel the same way ... then stay here with me, and let's see together where this path takes us. And please, *please* for the love of God, turn around so I can see what you're thinking, because I'm starting to feel like a blind man here-'

His voice broke off as I at last turned around, my hand falling softly away from the door handle. My coat and bag slipped unnoticed to the floor.

He was standing there, his arms spread wide as if asking – *would I run into them? Would I stay within their protective embrace?*

I think you can guess the answer I gave …

Chapter Twenty Eight

I've been on a journey ... a journey I never envisaged taking. A journey that, probably, in my own strength I wouldn't have dared to do.

And I've discovered so much; about those around me, about myself, about the emotions and complex feelings that can either cripple us... or release us.

I've been awoken to a new truth – that by letting my life hold a greater purpose, I have found a release from fear, and from a sense of worthlessness. That it's okay to allow something greater than you to take control, to shape and mould you. That in truth its the best thing you may ever do; though not always the easiest.

I've experienced a revelation ... that I'm far stronger and more courageous then I believed, or felt. We all are. I have literally gone into the shadows of myself and cast them out to discover who I really am.

We can't know what we are capable of unless we are challenged, taken out of our comfort zone, and forced to rely on gut feeling alone that *this just feels right.*

So I'm not going to allow myself to go back to what I was. Instead I'm going to embrace this new me. I may get hurt, I may make mistakes. But I'll keep on trusting, in those I love and who love me. And I will love without restraint, without barriers, but always understanding that even those we love may sometimes let us down or make the wrong decisions, that no one person alone can fulfil our every need apart from the one who looks down on us.

I have finished one journey...

Now it's time to begin the next.

THE END

Printed in Great Britain
by Amazon

41264895R00119